Take Me

Duff Coven: Book

2

M/M Paranormal

Romance

Jayda Marx

Author's Note

Thank you for your interest in my book! This low angst, **insta-love** paranormal romance features my take on some seriously sexy vampires. They share many attributes of vampires found in other fictional works, but not all. This book is the second in the Duff Coven series, and the books are best when read in order.

This title contains steamy scenes between fated mates, and moments so sweet they'll make your teeth tingle. My stories feature **relationships on the fast track**. I want my readers to finish my books with a smile on their face and a fierce case of the warm and fuzzies. Laughter is guaranteed, and each read delivers its own type of drama. Thanks again for taking a look and happy reading!

For my fellow Americans, I've included the definitions for some Scottish terms you'll find in the book. Enjoy!

Jumper - sweater

Puggled - worn out

Shite - shit

Football - soccer

Garden - yard (like front yard, back yard, etc.)

"Shut yer pus" - shut up

Crisps - potato chips

Bins - garbage cans

Tablet - similar to fudge, but it is more brittle with a grainy texture

Sweeties - sweets/candy

Brilliant - great/awesome

Mate - friend (unless it's a *vampire* mate)

Trainers - sneakers

Biscuits - cookies

Cheers - thanks

Sláinte - health, "Cheers!"

Dobber - idiot

Ma/Da - Mom/Dad

Clarty - dirty

Ya mangled fud - 'you misshapen vagina'

Chapter One

Lennox

"Thank you again for this, Dr. Adams," I told the man from the passenger seat of his car.

"Lennox, now that we're away from the center, you may call me Malcolm. We're friends, aren't we?"

I beamed as I nodded my head, and Dr. - no, *Malcolm* - smiled back. It was nice to finally have a friend. I'd spent the last four years feeling lonely and isolated, and battling the depression that tried to swallow me in the night.

Things weren't always this way. I was once a happy-go-lucky kid who loved to make people laugh. I was the class clown at my school, but I also worked hard to get good marks. It meant so much to me to see the proud smiles on my parents' faces when they congratulated me. They always made me feel so damn special. At the end of each semester, they'd take me out for a special dinner and let me choose whatever dessert I liked. I loved sweeties.

It was on one of our celebration nights that my life changed forever. My parents were taken from me in a terrible accident that still haunted my dreams. When my eyes closed at night, the scene replayed in my mind; the headlights, the sound of crunching metal, me screaming for my parents to wake up but getting no reply.

"Your smile is gone," Malcolm stated in a firm voice. "You know I like it better when you smile."

"Sorry." He always wanted me to smile; who wants their friends to be sad? I didn't want to upset him, so I forced my lips to curve up. Malcolm gave me a stiff nod and turned his attention back to the road ahead of us.

I first met Malcolm shortly after the accident. I was fourteen at the time and had just gone through the worst trauma I could imagine. Not only losing my parents, but what happened afterwards; visits through the court system, trying to figure out where

I'd go. I had no other family; my grandparents had passed years before, and neither my ma nor da had siblings. In the end, it was decided that I'd go to a boy's home.

Within my first week of living at St. Joseph's, I was required to meet with Malcolm - Dr. Adams - a psychologist who visited the home monthly to meet with boys who needed help.

At first, I wouldn't speak to him. I wouldn't speak to anyone. I didn't want to eat or do my schoolwork or chores. I couldn't sleep, but I didn't want to be awake. I was simply existing, even though I didn't necessarily want to do that either.

Instead of monthly visits, Dr. Adams visited me every day for a whole week, trying to get me to talk. He offered me toys or prizes if I'd speak to him, but I wasn't interested. Until one day he tempted me with a butter tablet. I was so hungry, and St. Joseph's only offered 'healthy' foods, and tablets were my favorite sweeties...so I agreed to talk.

But it was too hard to talk about my parents. I begged him not to make me, and he agreed that we could talk about whatever I liked. We discussed school subjects, animals, foods...everything except what we were 'supposed' to discuss. But Dr. Adams said it was a good place to start.

From then on, we met every month, and he didn't make me talk about things that upset me. Instead, he helped me with my schoolwork, smuggled in special treats for me, or even brought video games for us to play together. Our visits became something I looked forward to, and he said he enjoyed our time together too.

A couple of times, I *did* try to talk about my parents or the dreams I was having, but Dr. Adams said that it made *him* too sad to think about it. He called me his smiley boy, and that I brought happiness into his life. I didn't want to disappoint him, so I changed the subject and didn't bring it up again.

One day, Dr. Adams told me that I looked tense. I was; I had a secret that was getting too heavy to carry. I never told anyone because my parents passed before I figured things out and got the chance, and I was too scared of what others might do; St. Joseph's had strict rules and expectations, and most of the other boys who lived there were bigger and louder than I was, and some of them scared me. Being around the ones who *didn't* scare me only made my secret heavier.

Dr. Adams told me that sharing secrets could be fun; especially between friends. He rubbed my shoulders to make me feel more comfortable and offered me a plate of biscuits if I shared my secret. And so

I did; I whispered to him that I liked boys instead of girls.

I was afraid he'd be mad at me, or that he'd tell the nuns who ran the home. I was scared of them too. But Dr. Adams just smiled and said that he understood because *he* liked boys too. He made me promise not to tell; he said his career could be in danger if I did, and I didn't want him to get in trouble. He also said that I could be in danger if I told any of the other boys about myself, so I swore my silence and he swore his.

Since that day, I began seeing Dr. Adams differently; as a friend, or even a father figure. He was older than my own father was when he passed; Malcolm was in his late fifties and had gray, balding hair and thick glasses. But it was nice that he still wanted to be my friend even though I was young. He said we had a special connection.

It must be very special, because a few months ago, he approached me with an offer; St. Joseph's would no longer house me once I came of age. They didn't have the funding, and used what they *did* have on children who needed housing the most. I was worried about where I would go or what I would do, but Malcolm offered me a place at his home. He said that I could stay with him until I found my footing.

Of course, it was a secret too; he said no one could know about our arrangement, and I had no intention of telling. I was so grateful to him, and now, on my eighteenth birthday, I sat in the front seat of his car on my way to my new (though temporary) home.

My smile turned genuine when Malcolm pulled into a long gravel drive that led to a two story brick house. It was larger than the home I grew up in, and it had a huge garden surrounding it in every direction. During my time in fitness class at St. Joseph's, I discovered a liking for football; maybe Malcolm had a ball I could kick around his lawn.

When he parked the car, I jumped out onto the drive, tossing my backpack over my shoulder. I only owned a couple of outfits that St. Joseph's was able to supply, but they were enough.

A sharp sound to my left made me whip my head around, and my heart fluttered when I saw a small, scruffy gray dog tied to a rope in the garden. I'd always wanted a dog; they were so sweet and playful.

I opened my mouth to ask Malcolm if I could pet his pup, but before I got the words out, he yelled, "Shut yer pus, Freddie, or I'll beat yer arse!" in a harsher tone than I'd ever heard him speak. I flinched and the dog whimpered as it backed up to hide in its little house.

Malcolm's face relaxed when he saw how startled I was. He squeezed his hands on my shoulders and said, "Don't mind him; he's always noisy." I nodded, unsure what else to do; he didn't *actually* hit the dog. Maybe I was reading too much into the moment. "Now, where's my smile?" I released the breath I was holding and tipped my lips up. "Much better." He squeezed my shoulders again before dropping his hands.

"I can't wait to see your home," I said, changing the subject.

"It's your home too," he insisted, and my smile spread a little. "But before you come in, I need to set up a very special surprise."

"For me?" I asked as my heart raced.

"It *is* your birthday, isn't it? Why don't you wait right here while I get things ready?"

"Can I pet Freddie?" I asked hopefully, and Malcolm shot an irritated glance in the direction of the doghouse before shrugging.

"I suppose so, but don't let him off of his rope."

"Thank you!"

Malcolm disappeared through his front door and I sprinted over to the small wooden doghouse. I lowered onto my knees to look inside; I couldn't see Freddie in the shadows, but I heard his whimpers.

"It's okay, buddy," I crooned. "I'm sorry you got yelled at. Malcolm is probably nervous because I'm visiting for the first time. I think I have something to make it up to you." I dug around in my backpack until I found a half-eaten bag of crisps. I pulled one out and held it just inside the doghouse. "Do you want one?"

Freddie's nose appeared in the sunshine and twitched as it sniffed the treat. He gobbled it down greedily, making me smile. "If you come out a little more, I'll give you another one." I shook the bag and he stepped out of his house.

"It's okay," I told him again when he tucked his ears back at the sight of me. "I'm not going to hurt you." I poured some crisps in my hand and beamed when he ate them, his tongue tickling my palm.

"There you go, Freddie." When he was finished, I wiped my slobbery hand on my jeans. "Can I pet you? I'll be gentle." I inched my hand closer to him. He lowered his head, but he didn't back away. And when I brushed my fingers lightly across his head, his mouth dropped open and his tongue flopped out as his tail wagged back and forth.

"Oh, do you like that?" I scratched behind his wiry dark gray ears as he panted and wiggled. "What a good boy you are." I giggled when he came closer to me, bumping his head against my arms to get more love.

When I ran my fingers down his scruffy back, I felt something like a thick cord beneath his fur. "What is that?" I separated his hair and found a long, mounded scar down his back. "Did you have surgery, little guy?" I examined him closer and saw that he didn't have just one scar, but many spread across his flesh.

"What happened to you?" I asked as Freddie climbed onto my lap and curled into a ball. I wondered if Malcolm rescued him from a shelter or a bad home. I wondered how someone could mistreat an innocent little animal as I pet the precious pup. "I'm glad you're safe now."

Freddie was almost asleep when the front door of Malcolm's house opened and his voice called out, "Lennox, come inside for your surprise!"

"I've gotta go, buddy," I told Freddie with one last scratch behind his ears. "I'll come back out to see you later." He pawed at my legs when I stood up, wanting more attention and pulling at my heartstrings, so I poured the rest of my crisps out onto the ground for him before sneaking back to the house while he munched.

"I love your dog," I told Malcolm when I reached him at the front door.

"You'll love what I've got for you even more." I noticed that he'd taken off his shoes and unbuttoned half of the clasps on his dress shirt. He was at his home, and I figured he wanted to be comfortable. "Close your eyes."

I pinched my eyelids shut, excited for my birthday gift, and Malcolm took me by the hand. He led me down a long, straight hall as my brain spun with possibilities; maybe it was a football or some books or new clothes. Whatever it was, it wasn't necessary; he was doing so much for me already. A roof over my head was more than enough gift for *every* birthday.

We turned a corner and Malcolm pulled my backpack off my shoulders before whispering, "Open your eyes."

They sprung open in excitement, but my stomach knotted up at what I saw; he'd led me into a bedroom, where candles burned on nightstands and a dresser, and flower petals were scattered across the mattress.

He rested his hands on my shoulders and rubbed them, but it didn't feel as innocent or relaxing as it normally did. "What do you think?" he asked in my ear.

"I...I don't understand." I stepped away from him, but he followed.

"Don't you see? We can finally be together. There aren't any prying eyes or whispering lips around; it's just you and me. I brought you here so that we can live the life we've wanted." I froze in shock when he wrapped his arms around my waist from behind and grappled for the button on my jeans. "I've waited so long for this moment; do you know how many times I've pictured it? How often I've touched myself, pretending it was you? For four long years I've waited to get you alone, and now you're finally here."

Nausea settled in my gut at his words; four years ago I was a child. Even now that I was of age, this was still highly inappropriate; he was supposed to be my doctor - my mentor.

I forced air through my tight throat to tell him, "Malcolm, I can't. This isn't right. I need to leave."

Malcolm spun me roughly in his arms and stared at me with cold eyes. His jaw rippled as it clenched and fear bolted through me. I'd never seen him like this. "You're not going anywhere."

"Malcolm, please," I begged, putting my hands up in front of my chest. "You've got the wrong idea about us. You're my friend and-" I stopped speaking when his palm slapped across my cheek.

"You're not going to take this moment from me," he growled. "Not after you've teased me for years; flirting with me and flaunting your perfect little body in front of me when you knew I couldn't have a taste." He dug his fingernails into my shoulders and hauled me forward until our noses touched. "Well now I'm starving."

My body trembled with fear as I tried to reason with him. "I didn't mean to tease you. I thought we were just friends!" I'd never felt more stupid in my life; red flags had waved in my face for years, but I was just noticing them for the first time. Dr. Adams had been grooming me, *using* me, and now he was obsessed with a fantasy he'd apparently had for years. He was crazed and wouldn't stop until the fantasy was a reality.

He shoved me hard, knocking me back onto his bed and looming over me. "I brought you here. I'm giving you a home. You fucking owe me. I didn't want it to come to this, but this is happening one way or another."

He reached into his pocket and pulled out a syringe. His eyes were wild as he ripped the cap off with his teeth and spit it across the room. "This is a powerful paralytic from my office. You'll be mine to do with as I please; totally motionless, but you'll feel everything. You'll feel my love. Remember, *you're* forcing me to use this. I wanted our first time to be special. We could've had something beautiful. But I *will* have you, and I'll tape your lips up into a smile if I have to."

He climbed onto the bed, trapping my knees down with his. He lifted the needle and my fighting instincts kicked in. I grabbed his hand with both of mine, trying to pry the syringe from his fingers. Malcolm pressed his other palm into my face, pushing down with all of his strength until my nose ached and my eyes watered.

I thrashed my head, trying to shake him loose, but he only squeezed tighter. I clawed at his fingers until I broke skin and his blood trickled onto my hand. He flashed a look of pure rage before leaning down and biting my wrist. I cried out as my hands instinctively recoiled.

Malcolm laughed as he turned my head and inched the needle closer to my neck. I begged and wriggled and squirmed the best I could until my left leg worked out from beneath his.

I jerked my knee, slamming it into his balls. Malcolm flinched and groaned as he dropped the syringe onto the bed. Before I even knew what I was doing, I wrapped my fingers around it and plunged the needle into his bicep. I pushed the plunger and watched as Malcolm's look of fury instantly faded and his body went limp on top of me.

I pressed my fingers to the side of his throat (worried he was lying about what was in the syringe), feeling a weak but steady pulse. He was alive, but he was frozen in place.

I strained as I shoved his heavy dead weight off of my much smaller body. I stood up and ran my shaking hands through my hair as I looked over his still form. Everything hit me at once. *I missed the signs. I thought he was my friend. I thought he wanted to help me*. My stomach lurched when I thought about what he wanted to do to me. What if he *had* drugged me? What would he do with me after he fulfilled his fantasy? Would he get rid of me? Nobody knew I was there; he could have done anything to me and no one would know.

The possibilities were too horrible to think about. The only thing I knew for sure was that I had to get away. I didn't know how long the medicine would last in his system, so I had to move fast.

I scooped my backpack off of the floor and strapped it on as I ran at full speed out the front door. When my feet hit the grass, Freddie emerged from his doghouse, barking happily and wagging his tail at the sight of me.

Another realization punched me in the gut; Malcolm didn't save Freddie from anything. After seeing what he was going to do to me, I had no doubt the pup's scars came from the man's hand. Malcolm wasn't the saint he pretended to be; he was a monster, fueled by control and anger. I couldn't leave this poor creature to catch his wrath.

I jogged up to Freddie and unclasped his collar from around his neck. "Come on, buddy; you're coming with me." He attacked my chin with kisses as I zipped him up in my jacket so that he'd be warm and safe as we ran.

The problem was, I didn't know where we were running *to*. I had no home, no money, and I fed Freddie the last bit of food I had stashed away. My first thought was St.

Joseph's, but they wouldn't allow me *or* Freddie to stay. I wondered if I should warn them or even the police about what Dr. Adams did, but I was embarrassed to admit that I didn't realize what he was up to, and scared that he may blame everything on me. He was a respected professional and I was a homeless man with a troubled past; who would they believe?

I couldn't put my trust in anyone; look how that turned out. I had to rely on myself and do what was best for me and Freddie. And right now, that meant getting us far away from here.

Chapter Two

Lachlan

I groaned and kicked the blankets off of my body before standing up from my bed. I got plenty of sleep, as I only needed about two hours to be completely rested, but I was warm and comfortable, and not exactly keen on starting the day. But, I had a bakery to run.

Even though some days I wanted to stay in bed a little longer, I loved my job; baking treats and making stews and sandwiches for my Coven brought me happiness, and I enjoyed visiting with everyone while they ate. I especially loved speaking with my Coven Master Callum and his mate Brodie, whom he met nearly a year ago. They were my best friends in the world.

Brodie had been such a blessing to the coven. He'd lived through some terrible things, but kept a positive outlook. He had compassion and grace, and kindness towards everyone. There wasn't a single vampire in Beckenridge who didn't value his leadership as the Master's mate or call him a friend.

I called both Brodie and Callum my family. Callum and I had been close for half a millennium, fighting in battles side by side, and sharing life's ups and downs, and Brodie was like a little brother to me. But as much as I loved both of them and their company, sometimes it was difficult to watch them interact. They were so deeply in love and hid it from no one. Being without my fated mate, I couldn't help but yearn for the type of connection they shared.

I wanted to be someone's reason for smiling. I wanted to help carry their burdens and share in their joy. I craved to kiss away tears, laugh without limits and make love through the night. I longed to find and claim the other half of my soul and finally feel complete. It was hard to trust Fate and to be patient, but I had no other choice. I wouldn't seek out a superficial relationship with someone when I had my perfect match waiting for me somewhere. It would be an insult to me, my mate, and Fate herself.

I wrapped a black utility kilt around my waist, securing it at the side. I wore one nearly every day. I owned a few pairs of jeans, but I rarely wore them, opting for kilts instead; they were part of my heritage and culture, and I was proud to continue the tradition.

I pulled on a gray t-shirt and stepped into black boots before heading outside. The sky was pitch black, as the sun hadn't yet risen, but there were no stars to be seen; it had threatened to rain the past few days, but thus far all we'd seen were clouds.

It was chilly, but not cold enough for snow. The air around me pebbled my skin, but my thick frame was insulated with muscle and kept me from shivering. Plus, I knew once I was in the kitchen with a hot stove, I'd be plenty warm enough.

As I strolled through the cobbled streets, my attention was caught by movement in the distance. My vision was keen, even in low light, so I easily made out the source of the motion; a figure was on their knees in front of my bakery, sticking something slender in the knob of the front door as they wiggled it. *They're trying to break in!* Heaven help the man who wronged a vampire.

I was shocked (and a little impressed) when the door gave a soft *click* as it opened. But before the figure could step inside, I yelled, "Oi!" from the pit of my stomach. The person flinched and bolted away from me, but I didn't mind a chase.

I took off in the same direction, noticing that the person wasn't alone; a small dog stood its ground, yapping its head off at me until it got scooped into the person's arms.

When I reached the front of the bakery, it was if I ran into an invisible wall. My feet halted on their own and I dropped to one knee as a myriad of emotions overwhelmed me; fear, guilt, shame...yet none of them were my own, which could only mean one thing; I was near my mate, and experiencing his feelings through our empathic bond.

I breathed in deeply, inhaling the sweet scent of sugared vanilla; the scent of my mate. My heart beat quickly, pumping heated blood through my veins. My fangs lengthened and ached with desire for my beloved's flavor. My soul rejoiced at the long awaited recognition; I'd found my fated one. I no longer cared about his would-be burglary; all that mattered was getting closer to him.

I stood up and followed him, my mouth watering as his pheromones grew stronger the closer I got to him...but he was nowhere to be seen. Before I completely lost my shit, I was soothed by the sound of barking. *He's close.*

"Shh, Freddie," a sweet voice said in a soft tone, and I focused in on my mate's hiding spot amongst a collection of bins behind The Crown restaurant. Even without my sharp senses, I would've heard him. "Please, buddy; we have to be quiet or he'll find us."

I kept my steps quiet as I inched towards the pair; I didn't want to frighten my mate any more than he already was. But as I got closer, his anxiety and fear grew, saturating the air. This was something greater than the worry of being found.

"Freddy, I..." my mate said in a much weaker and more panicked voice than before. "I don't...feel...so good."

I gave up trying to be quiet and hustled over to where he was hiding. I tossed the bins aside and found my mate sitting on the ground with his back against the stone building. His chin was slumped onto his chest, and all I could see was the top of the black knit cap he wore on his head.

When I knelt on one knee and reached for him, his canine companion leapt at me, barking and snapping his teeth while raising the fur on the back of his neck to try to look intimidating. It was such a small thing, and I appreciated its attempt to protect my mate.

But, it would be a lot easier to care for him without an angry pup in my face, so I leaned in closer to Freddie, bared my fangs and let out a low but menacing growl. The dog quieted, flattened its fur, tucked its ears, and rolled over onto its back. I patted Freddie's stomach, acknowledging his submission and to show him that he had nothing to fear from me.

This time, Freddie gave me no opposition and only watched as I reached for my mate again. I cupped his cheek and carefully lifted his head, and my breath caught when I lay eyes on his beautiful face.

Long eyelashes fanned against his pale, smooth skin, and his cheeks were slender. He had the plumpest, pinkest lips I'd ever seen, and shaggy white-blond hair peeked out from beneath the hem of his cap.

Fate had blessed me with a stunning young man.

I quickly checked him over and found that his breathing was slow but even, and his pulse was fast but strong. I eased his eyelids open, stunned again by his pretty blue-gray irises, and thankful that his pupils weren't constricted.

He was okay; just passed out. He didn't appear to be on any substances or physically injured. Given his small frame, clammy skin, and the fact that he was trying to sneak into a bakery, I concluded that my poor mate was just very hungry. He probably burned up his last bit of energy running away from me.

My chest ached with guilt, but I'd make it up to him. I would care for him for all time, starting with getting him somewhere warm and comfortable and filling his belly.

I slid my forearm beneath his legs, settling it into the bends of his knees. I wrapped my other arm around his shoulders and gently lifted him from the ground, cradling him against my chest. His weight was slight, and though I wouldn't call him short, he was much smaller than my six foot three frame.

I turned to whistle for Freddie, but found that he was already next to my ankle, ready to follow. He stayed at my heels as I hustled through town back to my quaint stone home.

I gingerly removed my mate's bag from his back and lay him on the sofa before hurrying into the kitchen. I grabbed a bottle of honey from the pantry and a cloth from the drawer, which I dampened with cool water. When I made it back to the living room, I found Freddie curled up on my mate's lap.

"Good boy," I told him with a pat to his head. I wanted my man to have all the comfort he could get.

I sat on the edge of the sofa and slid the cap from my mate's head, smiling when his light hair fell in every direction. He looked precious and almost fragile as his body lay weak. With that and his white hair, he reminded me of a little lamb; meek, gentle, and lost. But I was here now to guide and care for him.

I draped the cool cloth across his forehead and pressed my thumb to his plump bottom lip, prying gently. When his mouth opened, I drizzled honey onto his gums and the tip of his tongue, hoping his body absorbed the sugar quickly to regain consciousness.

I combed my fingers through his wild hair while humming a quiet tune. *Come back to me, little lamb. Tell me your story.*

Chapter Three

Lennox

I groaned at the dizziness in my head and the gnawing ache in my stomach. I desperately needed food. Water had been easy enough to find, but Freddie and I hadn't eaten in nearly two weeks.

Oh god, Freddie! The last thing I remembered was running from a man who was chasing us away from the bakery. But what happened to Freddie? *Please let him be okay.* He was my only friend in the world, and I couldn't live with myself if he was in trouble. I tried to open my eyes, but groaned again at the light around me. *Damn, it must be morning already.*

"Shh, shh, take it easy, little lamb," a deep, soothing voice crooned as fingers combed through my hair. I relaxed at the soft touch for a moment before terror bolted through me. *Who the fuck is that?*

I forced my eyes open and though I had to squint to block out some light, I could still make out the face of the man leaning over me. God, he was gorgeous; he was ruggedly handsome with his cheeks thickly bearded with black hair. The matching hair on his head was short on the sides and a little longer on top, and a pair of striking emerald eyes glimmered back at me.

Wait, who cares if he's gorgeous? I was out cold and now I'm lying down with a stranger hovering over me. Thoughts of Malcolm infected my brain and I was terrified this guy was up to the same thing.

"Get away from me!" I yelled as I shoved the guy's chest as hard as I could. It was no good; he was a solid wall of muscle. Even though I couldn't move him on my own, he backed away as his eyes widened. "What did you do to me?"

"Nothing, I swear!"

I took a survey of my body; nothing felt injured, but there was a warm weight on my groin. "Liar! Don't touch me!" I went to swipe his filthy hand off of me, but instead, my fingers brushed against fur. I looked down and saw Freddie lying on my lap and staring back at me with worried eyes. "Freddie!" I scooped him into my arms and wiggled my way off of the sofa.

But when I stood up, my legs trembled beneath me and I dropped to my knees. "What did you do? What did you give me?" Did he have access to medications like Dr. Adams?

"Just a little honey," he replied, raising his hands in front of his chest. *Honey?* I searched my brain for the nicknames I'd heard some of the boys at St. Joseph's say when talking about drugs they'd tried, but 'honey' didn't come to mind. The man gasped. "You're not allergic, are you?"

What? It was then that I noticed the subtle sweetness in my mouth. I licked my teeth and quickly placed the flavor. "Wait...you mean *actual* honey?"

He nodded. "You looked like you needed sugar."

I flinched when something fell from my head and landed on Freddie's back. I quickly lifted it off of him and realized that it was a damp rag. I looked back at the man and asked confusedly, "Why were you helping me?"

He rubbed his chest for a moment like the question somehow hurt him before he slowly knelt on the floor in front of me. "I'm sorry that I frightened you. I just saw someone trying to break into my bakery and

I reacted. But when I found you, I realized that you just needed something to eat. So I brought you here until you woke up, and now I'd like to make you some breakfast."

This can't be real. Am I dreaming? Maybe I'm dead. No, I felt Freddie's warm weight in my arms and the breath in my lungs. *This guy has to be a hallucination, though; a delusion crafted by a food deprived mind.* No, I'd felt his body and his strength when I shoved him. *Shit, he helped me and I shoved him.*

"I'm sorry I pushed you; erm, *tried* to push you," I offered. "I was just scared." The man smiled and I got dizzy all over again when his eyes sparkled and his skin bunched up in soft creases.

"I understand, but you don't have to be afraid now. You can trust me."

I wanted to; something deep inside me said that I could, and *should*, but I'd been fooled before. I knew how quickly friendly eyes could burn with fury, or how kind words could turn hateful. This man was much bigger than Malcolm; if he turned on me, I'd have no chance. The best thing to do was keep my guard up, stay alert, and protect myself.

When I didn't reply, the man stood up and offered me his hand. "Let's get you something to eat." That was an offer I couldn't refuse; my survival depended on it, so I clasped his fingers, noticing that his hand dwarfed mine. He didn't jerk me up or hurry me along; he just lended me his strength and support as I rose to my feet. Once I was standing upright, my head spun again and my knees buckled.

"I've got you," he said as he caught me before I hit the floor again. I knew I was on the small side, but he carried me through his home like I weighed nothing. Guilt and contentment warred inside me; while I admittedly liked the feel of being held in his arms, he was caring for me and doting on me when I didn't even know his name.

"Here we are," he announced when we arrived in his kitchen. It was warm and homey, decorated in dark woods and red and green plaid. He pulled out a tall chair from beneath a bar and helped me into it.

"Steady?" I nodded; as long as I was sitting down, I seemed to be okay.

The man took Freddie from my arms and I assumed he was going to put him on the floor, but he surprised me by pulling out the chair next to me and settling him in it. "There you go, pup; I bet you could use some breakfast too." I appreciated him looking after me, but his care for Freddie was what truly warmed my heart.

"Who *are* you?" I asked before realizing how rude it sounded. Before I could apologize, the man did.

"Forgive me, little lamb; I was so focused on your safety, I forgot my manners." He held out his hand and said,

"My name is Lachlan McKay, and it is my greatest honor to meet you."

I tucked my hand inside his again, loving the way it enveloped me in warmth. I figured giving him just my first name couldn't do much harm, so I replied, "I'm Lennox," though I was personally a fan of 'little lamb'. I'd never had a pet name, and it sounded so sweet coming from Lachlan's lips.

"Lennox," he repeated, and a shiver travelled down my spine at the sound of my name spoken in his deep voice. "That's beautiful." Before I could thank him, Lachlan dropped my hand and hurried around to the other side of the counter. "Here's something to hold you over while I'm cooking." He slid something towards me, and my heart skipped a beat when I realized it was a large square of butter tablet.

"This is my favorite sweetie." I took a huge bite and hummed at the flavor.

"Do you like it? I made it myself."

"It's delicious," I answered through a full mouth. I broke off a piece and fed it to Freddie, who was pawing at my thigh, before I crammed another bite past my lips.

"Easy, there," Lachlan told me with a gentle smile. My cheeks flushed when I realized what a pig I was being.

"Sorry," I said, placing the rest of the tablet on the countertop. "That was rude of me." I'd gotten a ruler to the back of the knuckles more than once for being too excited or grabby when it came to food, but I guess I didn't learn.

"No, no, not at all," Lachlan insisted as he put his hand on mine. "Please eat all you like; it thrills me that you like my baking. I just don't want you to get ill by eating too quickly after being with an empty stomach for so long."

Relief washed over me until I realized what he said. He knew I'd been hungry for a while. My cheeks flushed when I asked, "How could you tell?", as if my hoggish eating wasn't clue enough.

He answered with a sad smile, "You looked pretty sick." He squeezed my hand

and asked, "What happened to you, little lamb?"

I wanted to tell him, but I was afraid; what if he knew Dr. Adams and sent me back to him? What if I told Lachlan my story, but he didn't believe me? What if he did, but he blamed *me*? What if he thought I was too dirty or too pitiful and took away his aid? I needed food. Freddie needed food. I couldn't mess up this opportunity. "I, erm...I'd rather not talk about it."

"I understand," he replied, but I didn't miss the sadness in his eyes. "But I'm here if you ever do." I nodded and he lightly slapped the counter when he dropped my hand. "*So*, breakfast. Let's see what we've got."

Lachlan turned away from me and searched through his refrigerator. I only stared at his arse a little, and I only tried to peek up his kilt once (I was curious what he was wearing under there, but I couldn't get a good look). I'd always loved a man in a kilt, but Lachlan put all other men I'd seen to shame. His broad frame and thick, hairy legs were *made* to be shown off in the manly garb.

When he turned around to face me again, I quickly snapped my eyes away, hoping he didn't notice me peeping. I didn't want to offend him or make him angry. Judging by his kindness and the pet name he gave me, I could *assume* some things about Lachlan, but I didn't *know* that he was gay. I didn't think it was polite to ask, so I kept my questions to myself while Freddie and I finished off the tablet (with smaller bites).

Lachlan placed a package of bacon and a carton of eggs on the counter, along with a large silver bowl. My eyes were fixed on his hands as he cracked a full dozen eggs into the bowl, and my gaze crawled up his arm as he beat them. The muscles of his forearm bulged as he stirred, but the rest of his body didn't even jiggle. Just *watching* him cook was a feast in itself.

I jerked my eyes away again when Lachlan cleared his throat. "Will you tell me a little about yourself?" he asked in a voice that sounded huskier than before.

"Oh...okay." Not wanting to give too many details, I offered only, "I turned eighteen a couple of weeks ago."

A wide smile crossed his lips. "Well, happy belated birthday."

"Thanks," I answered tightly; my birthday had been anything but happy. "So...how old are you?" I was utterly terrible at small talk.

"You wouldn't believe me if I told you," Lachlan replied with a wink.

"Try me."

He leaned forward and whispered as if it were a secret, "Four hundred eighty nine."

I snorted and rolled my eyes. "You're right, I don't believe you." I really couldn't blame him for teasing me, though; I wasn't being forthright about myself either. I wanted to know more about him, though, so I asked, "Have you always lived here?"

"Aye." He bent below my line of vision and when he stood back up, he was holding a skillet. "I love this village. I've lived here all of my life."

"All four hundred eighty nine years of it?" I teased back, and his smile widened.

"Exactly."

Freddie and I both licked our lips when he peeled open the package of bacon. He pointed down at the strips and asked, "Do you like it fried crispy or soft?"

"Hell, I don't care; I'd eat it raw."

Lachlan laughed, the soft rumble warming me from the inside. *Get a grip, Lennox!* I'd never felt like this before; I'd known the man all of fifteen minutes since he scraped me off of the ground, but I was drawn to him. I liked Lachlan.

My feelings towards him weren't the same as any other curiosities or fantasies I'd had before. This was different. I wanted to know everything about him. I wanted him to carry me and hold me in his arms again. I wanted to curl up in his lap and tell him everything about my past so that he could ease my pain. My heart knew that he could. But how? How was this possible? It couldn't be. Maybe I was just so desperate for human interaction that my mind was forming emotions that weren't really there. They sure felt real, though.

Lachlan turned away from me to face the stovetop, but he spoke to me over his shoulder as he spread bacon onto the skillet. "What do you like to do for fun?"

"I like playing football."

"Really?" He looked back at me with a toothy grin. "I love football; watching *and* playing."

"Maybe you and I could play together some time," was out of my mouth before I could stop it. I held my breath; as far as I knew, Lachlan could be planning on feeding me bacon and kicking me out of his house, which was more than fair. But here I was clumsily asking him to spend more time with me.

I sighed in relief when he answered, "I'd love that." With another peek at me, he asked, "Does Freddie like to play ball too?" The dog's ears perked up at his name.

"Oh, erm...I'm not sure." When Lachlan gave me a curious look, I explained, "I've only had him for a couple of weeks." *After I stole him.*

"Was he a birthday gift?"

I looked down at the counter and squirmed in my seat when I replied, "You could say that." I hated lying to him. I hated lying *period*, but something about being dishonest with Lachlan made my stomach turn. I shifted the focus back to him by asking, "What else do you like to do besides football?"

"I love baking and cooking; I love it so much that I made a career out of it." My stomach squeezed again, this time with guilt over trying to steal from Lachlan's bakery. Granted, I was fueled by hunger and need, but it was still a shite thing to do. "Plus, I love getting together with friends, fishing, seeing movies, attending festivals...I guess there isn't much that I *don't* like."

"I used to love going fishing."

He looked back at me again. "Used to?"

"I haven't been in a long time," I shrugged. "My father used to take me salmon fishing at Loch Tay when I was younger, but..." I didn't finish my story; it was too painful to talk about, and I didn't want to get upset in front of Lachlan.

He didn't push me to speak, and the only sound in the kitchen was sizzling bacon for several long moments before he said, "There's great salmon fishing at Loch Kilgore. It's only about twenty kilometers from here; maybe that's something else we can do together."

His words lifted my spirits, and for the first time in a long time, thinking about the activity filled me with excitement instead of grief. I answered honestly, "I'd like that."

"Brilliant." He turned a couple of knobs on the stovetop before grabbing a stack of plates out of the cupboard. Once he filled them, he turned around and served me a plate full of steaming scrambled eggs and a pile of bacon.

When he scooted a second plate in front of Freddie, which only held bacon strips, Freddie licked Lachlan's hand before putting his little paws up on the counter and digging right in. "You're welcome, pup," Lachlan said with a chuckle.

"He really likes you," I told Lachlan as I lovingly watched Freddie chow down. "He's scared of most people and just barks at them, but he trusts you."

"Dogs are great judges of character," he replied with a wink. *Maybe I* can *trust him.* "What would you like to drink? I have tea, milk, or orange juice."

"Orange juice sounds great."

Lachlan collected two glasses of orange juice and a bowl of water for Freddie. "May I sit by you?" he asked me as he carried his plate around to my side of the bar. I nodded and when he settled in beside me, my pulse raced. Something as simple as just being near him sent me for a loop.

I distracted myself with a big bite of eggs, followed by a strip of bacon. His cooking was incredible and I had to remind myself to eat slowly. "This is delicious," I told him between bites. "You're a great chef."

"Thanks, but it's hard to mess up eggs." On top of being kind and thoughtful, he was also humble.

He was the whole damn package and before a second thought, I asked, "Are you married?" *Fuck, did I actually say that?* My cheeks burned as I took a long sip of juice.

"Naw. I've been waiting for the right man to come along."

Man? He said man! I barely swallowed my juice without spitting it all over the counter in excitement. Even though he didn't ask, I told him, "I'm gay too!" in the most awkward way possible. Since I'd hidden my sexuality from most people, I had *zero* experience in flirting.

I kept waiting for Lachlan to laugh or blatantly tell me he wasn't interested in anything I was offering (or *trying* to offer, even though I didn't know what the hell I was doing) but he did neither. He just looked at me seriously and asked, "Are you involved with anyone?"

Damn if the man didn't look saddened by the question. *Why* was anyone's guess; I was homeless, running, and had literally nothing to offer. Of course, Lachlan didn't know those things since I hadn't told him anything about myself. All I'd done thus far was try to rob him, lied to him, and eaten his food.

I wanted to slam my head on the bar, but instead, I replied, "No, I'm not dating anyone." He smiled and it looked so nice that I wanted to make him smile more. "I've *never* dated anyone, or...you know...*been* with anyone." *Wait, was that a weird thing to say?*

Maybe, because Lachlan's smile disappeared and his eyes changed; they went...*darker* somehow, and his jaw clenched when he swallowed. *Well, damn, I've ruined this.* I didn't know how to make things better; I could tell him that I knew all about sex and that I'd done *plenty* of things to myself, but that didn't seem like appropriate breakfast conversation.

Before I could say *anything*, Lachlan spoke up, his voice husky again. "Have you ever been kissed, little lamb?" Even though I was embarrassed of my answer, I didn't want to outright lie to him anymore, so I slowly shook my head no.

"I'd like to be." Lachlan's gaze drifted down to my lips as my heart leapt...and then dropped. As much as I wanted to kiss him, I couldn't. Because I was afraid he wouldn't want to if he knew more about me, but I wasn't ready to talk about things to find out. "You know...one day," I added in a whisper.

I worried Lachlan would be mad, or accuse me of teasing him like Malcolm said, but he did neither; he just gave me a gentle smile. He cupped his hand on my shoulder and I gave a quiet gasp at the peace that came with his touch. It felt as if he was opening my heart and filling it with understanding and care. *How is he doing that?*

"Then I hope one day I'm lucky enough to be the one who gets to kiss you." My heart swelled and my lips turned up. I'd never met anyone like Lachlan; he made me feel incredible. "I love your smile." My stomach lurched and my face dropped as I remembered the words Malcolm told me for years. "I'm sorry; did I say something wrong?"

I shook my head because he *hadn't* said anything wrong; it was a very nice compliment and it was my hang up to deal with. I guiltily turned back to my breakfast and shoveled in some more eggs as I tried to come up with a way to discuss what happened to me.

Thanks to Malcolm's obsession and misdirection, I had no idea *how* to talk to people. He never wanted to hear about my troubles. And if a fucking psychologist didn't want to hear about them, why would Lachlan? I didn't want to sound whiny or irritating. I was lost, confused, and filled with pain I didn't know how to express.

Lachlan didn't say a word; he just gently pat my back and let me think. As he tapped me in a steady rhythm, the same peace and comfort from before flowed through me. His quiet confidence and support meant the world to me, but I wasn't sure how to thank him.

Freddie gave a bark and I looked over to see that his plate and water bowl were empty. "Are you full, buddy?" I picked him up off of his chair and chuckled at how round his stomach was. "Looks like it."

"What about you, Lennox?" Lachlan questioned, eyeballing my own empty plate. "Did you get enough to eat? I can make you something else if you like."

"I'm stuffed, but thank you." He nodded his head as he gave a proud smile. I pushed out my chair to put Freddie on the floor, but gasped when I saw where he'd been sitting. "Oh no! Freddie got mud all over your chair and counter. I'm so sorry, Lachlan; I didn't know he was that dirty."

I looked down at myself and saw that I wasn't exactly clean either. I'd rinsed my face off in the streams we drank from (I would have climbed in if it weren't so cold out), but my clothes were a right mess. "I guess I *should* have known since we've been sleeping outside, but-" *Fuck; didn't meant to say that.*

I snapped my eyes to Lachlan and found him rubbing his chest again. "Don't worry about the mud," he said, waving his other hand. "It's no trouble. But Lennox, you can't be sleeping outside and not eating. Please stay with me. I have a bed for you to use and I love to cook."

Although everything inside me was screaming for me to agree, I shook my head. "I can't. I don't have any money to pay you for the room and I can't take advantage of your kindness."

He sighed and gave me a sad smile. "You can't take advantage of something I'm offering freely. And I certainly don't want your money."

I hugged Freddie tighter to my chest when I asked, "What *do* you want?" I knew; I *knew* he wasn't like Malcolm, just from the way he spoke to me and made me feel, but I couldn't stop my fear from bubbling up to the surface.

"Just to help," he answered quietly. "I just want you to be safe." My heart filled with happiness, which only grew when Lachlan added, "And Freddie too, of course." Freddie and I were a package deal, and this wonderful man was accepting us both, with no strings attached.

"Thank you," I told him seriously. "I'd love to stay, and we'll try not to be too much trouble."

"That's not possible," he assured with a wink. "Now, it'll only take a minute for me to clean these dishes, and then would you like to help me give Freddie a wash?"

"Sure!" Not only would a warm bath feel nice for him, it would keep Lachlan's floors clean too.

Lachlan rinsed the dishes and loaded them into his dishwasher as I scrubbed Freddie's mess from the seat and counter, even though Lachlan said I didn't have to. Helping out was the *least* I could do after what he was offering us.

Lachlan filled his kitchen sink with warm, soapy water and I lowered Freddie into it. I chuckled when he snapped his teeth at the bubbles, and my heart melted when Lachlan shielded the pup's eyes when he rinsed his head. He was a big, strong man, but he was showing this little creature only gentility.

I laughed again when both of us lathered up Freddie until his body was completely covered with thick white suds. I explained, "Now *he* looks like a little lamb," and Lachlan chuckled along with me. We scrubbed and rinsed until Freddie was spotless.

"I'll go grab a towel," Lachlan offered. "Be back in a flash."

He left the room and I pet over Freddie's wet head. My heart ached when I saw how filthy his bath water was. I leaned down and told him quietly, "I'm sorry, buddy. I took you to save you, but then I couldn't even give you food or a clean, warm bed." I sighed and scratched behind his ears. "Thank god Lach found us, huh?" Freddie licked my forearm as I pet him, as if telling me he wasn't angry with me, and that everything would be okay.

"Here we go," Lachlan announced in a quiet voice when he re-entered the room carrying a thick red towel. He gave me a gentle smile and I wondered if he'd heard what I said. It didn't bother me if he did; Freddie and I *were* lucky to be with him.

I lifted Freddie from the water and Lachlan wrapped him in the towel, rubbing over every inch of his fur until he was dry and fluffy. When Lach put him on the floor, Freddie took off like a shot, running wildly through every room as we watched and laughed. Now that the pup was clean and full, he was an energetic little guy.

I became embarrassed again when I looked down at my soiled clothing and dirty hands. I kept my eyes down when I asked

Lachlan, "Would it be okay if I washed up too?"

"Of course." He pulled the plunger from the sink and dried his hands. "The bathroom's right down this hall." He motioned to his left, but I looked back into the living room.

"I *might* have something a little cleaner to wear in my bag."

"Why don't you let me put your things in the wash? I have a friend who lives close by and is about your size; I'm sure he wouldn't mind loaning you an outfit."

I didn't want to impose on *another* person, but dressing in dirty clothes after a shower wouldn't do me much good. "If you don't think he'd mind, I'd really appreciate it."

"Then I'll call him now and see if he'll come over."

I knotted my fingers together and asked, "Would it be rude if I didn't meet him right now?" I certainly didn't look my best, and I wasn't ready to answer questions he may have.

"Not at all," Lachlan assured me. "But when you *are* ready to meet him, I have a feeling you two will be the best of friends."

I hoped so. I'd love to stay here and form friendships (and maybe even something stronger with Lachlan). The longer I was around the nice man, the more

I wanted it. Though I hadn't known him long, I wanted to be part of his life and his world.

I gasped lightly when he put his hand on the small of my back to lead me down the hall. The simple touch warmed me through to my core.

"Is this okay?" he asked as he searched my eyes as if he were looking for hesitation.

"It's great." My knees weakened when he smiled at me, but somehow my legs carried me down the hall at his side.

Lachlan pushed open the bathroom door and flipped on the light, revealing the room that was decorated much like his kitchen; there was a dark wood vanity, white fixtures, and a plaid shower curtain. A fuzzy red mat lay on the floor outside of the shower.

"There's soap and clean washcloths in the shower," he offered, "And towels are under the sink. Would it be okay if I put the new outfit on the sink for you while you're showering? I won't come in." I nodded; he was being respectful of my boundaries while taking care of me. "Okay, I'll go make the phone call and you just yell if you need me."

He turned to leave the room, but stopped when I rested my hand on his back. "Lach?" He didn't recoil at the nickname; instead smiling sweetly when he faced me again. "Thank you for everything."

"It's my pleasure, little lamb." He cupped my cheek for the briefest moment, dropping his hand before I could react beyond my quickened pulse. "Relax and enjoy," he added before leaving the room, pulling the door shut behind him.

I let out a long breath and turned to start a stream of heavenly hot water.

Chapter Four

Lachlan

I've got to get a hold of myself. Being so close to my beautiful mate, I wanted to shower him with my affections. I wanted to kiss his sweet lips, and hold his beautiful body while he told me his secrets. But he'd made it clear that he wasn't ready for any of that yet, and the last thing I wanted to do was make him uncomfortable.

I sighed and hurried down the hall, excitedly pulling my phone from my pocket. I couldn't wait to tell Callum and Brodie about my good fortune. I dialed Callum's number and my friend answered on the first ring.

"Lachlan? Is something wrong?" I never called him this early, as I was usually busy with the bakery.

"No, Cal; everything is very, very right. I've found my mate! He's here in my home!"

"Seriously? Congratulations, Lach." There was a quiet rustle over the line, and Callum's voice said, "Brodie? Wake up, m'anam."

"Hmm?" Brodie gasped. "What's wrong?"

"Lach's found his mate!"

After another gasp, Brodie's voice crossed the line. "Lach, that's amazing! We're so happy for you! Where is he? What's his name? Can I meet him?"

I chuckled at his excitement. "He's in the shower at the moment. His name is Lennox, but I'm afraid he's not ready to meet anyone yet. I'm calling for a favor-"

"Anything," Callum's voice insisted.

"Lennox needs an outfit. He looks about Brodie's size and I hoped that-"

"Say no more," Brodie cut in. "I'm on my way."

The line went dead and I smiled down at my phone. My friends were incredible. It wasn't more than three minutes later when a knock sounded at my front door. I pulled it open and found the couple beaming from ear to ear. Brodie's curly hair was tousled from sleep and his shirt was half-tucked into his jeans from dressing quickly.

"Are these okay?" Brodie asked, holding out another pair of jeans and a folded black jumper.

"They're great, thank you." I barely had the clothing in my hands when Brodie threw his arms around my waist and squeezed.

"Lach, I'm so happy for you!"

"Congrats, my friend," Callum added as he slung an arm around my neck. "I *knew* you would find your fated one. I want to hear all about the man lucky enough to win your heart."

"He's beautiful and sweet, but reserved. I wish I knew more about him," I admitted. Brodie let me loose and looked up at me in question. "He's been through something terrible; I can feel it. He's scared and alone; well, except for Freddie."

"Who's Freddie?" Brodie asked curiously. I smiled and gave a sharp whistle. A moment later, paws slid across the wood floor until Freddie came into view. "Oh my god, he's adorable!" Brodie squealed, even though the pup was barking at him.

Brodie lowered to his knees and reached out just as Callum warned him, "Careful, m'anam." But as soon as Brodie touched Freddie's head, the pup melted, rolling onto his back and wagging his tail as he soaked up the love.

"Aw, he's just a sweetie, aren't you, wee one?" Brodie cooed as he pet the pooch's stomach, and Callum watched his mate with a dreamy grin.

He turned his smile to me and observed, "Your house will be full of love and excitement with your new little family."

My heart swelled at the incredible thought, but it still wasn't totally at ease. "I wish I knew Lennox's story," I admitted to him in a quiet voice. "He was hungry when I found him, Cal - and dirty. He let it slip that he'd been sleeping outside; he doesn't even have a place to call his home."

"He does now," Callum argued, and a smile spread across my face.

"Aye, he does now. But I want to do more. I want to care for him; to erase all of his troubles, but I need to know how to help."

"You're helping already," he insisted. "Give Lennox your strength and your love. Let him know that you're here for him, but don't push him. He will feel the mate pull between you and you'll earn his trust. You are the finest man I know, and it won't be long before Lennox sees that for himself."

"Thank you," I replied seriously.

"And if you need anything at all, don't hesitate to call me."

"There is one thing you can help me with." He raised his brows and I explained, "I'm taking the day off from the bakery to spend with Lennox. Could you post a sign in the window for me?"

"You're finally taking a day off?" Brodie asked, looking up at me with wide eyes. "Lennox *must* be pretty great."

"He is."

"We'll take care of it," Callum agreed. He patted my back before looking down at Brodie, who was loving all over the pup again. "We better get going, m'anam. Lachlan needs to tend to his mate."

Brodie nodded and gave Freddie one last pat down. "I hope I see you again soon, buddy." He stood up and wrapped me in another hug. Brodie was very tactile with his friends; he'd been denied physical attention all of his life until he met Callum, and now he eagerly shared it with those whom he held dear. "Please tell Lennox that I'm happy he's here, and that I can't wait to meet him."

"I will." After I gave him a squeeze, Brodie took Callum's hand and they left my house with a wave.

I hurried down the hall and after making sure the shower was still running, I opened the bathroom door only enough to slide the clothing inside, resting them on the edge of the sink before shutting the door again.

I mosied back into the living room and glanced out the window; it was growing lighter as the morning ticked by, but there was still no sunshine to be found. Light gray clouds filled the sky and I wondered if we'd actually see some rain.

I heard the bathroom door open down the hall, and I turned around to see Lennox walking towards me. He looked stunning; his skin was pink from the hot water and his damp hair was combed but still messy. Brodie's clothes fit him nicely, except that the jeans were a few inches too short. But Lennox capped the hems of the legs, giving the denim a trendy appearance. "You look beautiful."

My heart ached when he looked over his shoulder to see who I was speaking to, but I smiled when realization hit him and he ducked his head while his cheeks pinked even more.

"Thank you. Erm, where can I put these?" He held up his dirty clothes from earlier.

"I'll take them. If you get your other outfits, I'll wash them as well." I didn't want to go through his bag without him. Lennox nodded and collected his clothes, and I put them all in the wash. When I joined him again, I told him, "Brodie asked me to tell you how happy he is that you're here. He and his husband Callum are looking forward to meeting you." His surprise and delight filled the air at the word husband, and I put together that he'd not been around many others with his same desires.

"That was very nice of them," he replied before drumming on his thighs. "So...when do you need to be at work? You said you owned the bakery and I know that's where you were going...when you found me."

His guilt filled the room and I wanted to cheer him up, so I said, "I've decided to take the day off."

"Oh." His eyes drifted to the floor."I understand." *I* didn't understand his sadness until he added, "I know I haven't given you any reason to, but you can trust me in your house alone. I swear I won't take anything.

But if you don't trust me, I can sit in the bakery while you work."

"Oh Lennox, no." Unable to stop myself, I stepped toe to toe with him and cupped both of his cheeks in my hands, looking into his eyes to show him my sincerity. "I trust you fully, little lamb. I'm taking the day off to spend time with you...unless you'd rather have some time alone."

He shook his head in my hands. "I'd love to spend the day with you."

I soaked up the feeling of his soft, smooth skin for a few more seconds before dropping my hands. "Would you like to take Freddie for a walk through the village? I can show you around and he can get some fresh air." And I thought Lennox might be more comfortable if his friend joined us.

"That sounds really nice."

"Great. Are you ready to go now?"

"Sure."

I whistled for Freddie again, and he naturally followed my lead, staying right at my heels as Lennox and I left the house.

"It looks so old here," Lennox commented as we walked down the center path through town. He flinched and added, "I mean that in a good way. I like that it looks old; it's very beautiful." He sighed and I chuckled while patting his back.

"I love the old world charm here as well."

"Charming!" Lennox exclaimed.
"*That's* the word I was looking for." I smiled wider; *he* was charming and so damn cute.

"The village *is* very old; it was established over four hundred years ago. It looks much like it did then, though more businesses and homes have been built over time. Beckenridge is much smaller than the cities that surround us, but that's one thing I enjoy about it; we are all friends and kin here. We all look out for one another."

"That's so great," he replied with a grin. I was careful not to say it since it bothered him earlier, but I loved to see him smile. Not only was making him happy my sole purpose in life, but he looked gorgeous; his blue-gray eyes shined and his plump lips gave way to matching dimples on each cheek.

I knew I was staring, but I couldn't bring myself to look away; fine art was meant to be appreciated. And Lennox didn't seem to mind; he was staring right back at me. I felt no trepidation coming from him; only longing and intrigue.

My body craved him in every way; to caress every inch of his smooth skin, to taste his sweet lips, to feel his body tremble beneath my touch, but I would take things slow until he was ready. Hoping it wasn't too much, I took a deep breath and asked, "May I hold your hand while we walk?" Lennox gave a shy, pretty smile as he offered his hand, and I threaded our fingers together.

Affection and joy swelled within him when I gave his hand a squeeze and led him further down the path.

I showed him Evan's glass shop and the other businesses in the area as Freddie sniffed the doorways and trotted down the path. I pointed out the whiskey distillery and the old prison, a couple of pubs and The Crown. And finally, we came to my bakery, and Lennox's guilt was so thick, it was difficult to breathe.

"I'm sorry for what I did here," he told me quietly.

"Please don't worry about it; I understand. Besides, we were fated to meet, and I'm grateful for any way it happened."

Lennox gave me a curious look and asked, "You believe in fate?"

"Aye. Do you?"

He thought for a moment before shaking his head no. "I've heard that everything happens for a reason, but I don't buy it. Sometimes shitty things happen and no good comes from them; they only lead to more shitty things. And if there's some force planning out those things or making them happen, I don't want anything to do with it."

My heart broke for him. What happened to my sweet mate that hurt him so deeply? I brushed my thumb across his knuckles and told him, "I don't believe that every moment of our lives is mapped out. I think that there are unexpected twists and turns, and accidents or mistakes that do nothing but cause pain." He squeezed my hand for support, and he gasped quietly when I pushed my love and encouragement into him.

"But, I also believe that there are people whom we are destined to meet. They will help us through the tough times so that we're never alone, and they'll celebrate the good times with us, making them even sweeter. I believe that everyone has a perfect match fated to them who will soothe and complete their soul." It wasn't just my belief; I knew for a fact that every vampire was granted that match by Fate herself, and I'd finally found mine.

Lennox swallowed thickly. "So, do you think that fate brought *us* together?"

I smiled and squeezed his hand. "I believe it with all of my heart." Lennox didn't answer, but his emotions were going haywire. I was pelted with his hope, affection, need, and worry. I was grateful for our empathic link, because though his insides were going nuts, his outer appearance was calm and unmoving. I imagined he'd spent a lot of time not showing his feelings.

Though I longed to hear his troubles and help him through them, I wouldn't force him to talk about them. Instead, I gave his hand another light squeeze and said, "Come with me; I want to show you something."

I led Lennox beyond the outer limits of town, to a spot where he could see the rolling hills surrounding us, which the winter heather dotted with white and purple blooms. Long grass swayed in the gentle breeze, and I felt peace radiating from my mate. I knew he'd love this place; it was one of my favorites in the world. I often came here to soak up the beauty and serenity of nature.

Our final stop of the tour was the large grassy field where Callum first scented Brodie. I chuckled as I watched Freddie run and leap across it. "I know this may not look like much," I told Lennox, "But this field is very important to our village. We've held feasts, celebrations, weddings, and even Highland Games here on this land."

"It would be the perfect place for a football game."

I smiled and asked, "Would you fancy a game now?"

"Really? I'd love to play."

"Brilliant. I've got a ball at the house; why don't we take Freddie home to rest and we'll come back to play?"

"Sounds great." I whistled for Freddie and he zoomed back to my side as Lennox chuckled and shook his head.

The three of us walked back into the heart of town, to the string of quaint stone homes and people milling about on the walkways. Amongst them, heading towards their own home were Callum and Brodie, whom I assumed just got finished hanging the sign that I requested.

When they saw us, Callum beamed at our linked hands, and Brodie waved wildly over his head. Lennox's anxiety rose, and he squeezed my hand tighter and stepped closer to me. I loved that he drew comfort from me, but I didn't want him to be afraid.

"It's okay," I told him quietly. "That's Callum and his husband Brodie; they're my closest friends."

"He gave me these," he remembered, running his hand down his borrowed shirt.

"That's right. I know they'd love to meet you, but it's okay if you're not ready. They'll understand."

Lennox was quiet for several seconds before he let out a long breath. "I'd like to meet them. If they're your friends, I know they'll be nice." My heart fluttered, but went into overdrive when he added, "I want to meet the people who are important to you."

"Thank you, little lamb." A grin stretched across my face as I waved my friends over, and I chuckled at the sight of Brodie nearly dragging Callum across the street.

When they were close, Freddie jumped onto his back legs and pawed at Brodie's jeans for attention. "Be easy,

Freddie," Lennox commanded. "I'm sorry;
he's usually not like this with new people,"
he told Brodie.

"Oh, I don't mind. Besides, we met
earlier, so we're already friends." Brodie
scratched behind the pup's ears as Lennox
gave one of his breathtaking smiles. It
seemed that he approved of anyone who
was nice to his pooch. Brodie stretched out
his other hand and said, "I'm so happy to
meet you, Lennox. My name's Brodie."

"Good to meet you too," Lennox
replied, shaking hands. "Thanks for the
clothes."

"It was no trouble." Brodie dropped
Lennox's hand and introduced, "This is my
husband Callum." Being human himself, he

knew 'husband' was the easiest way to explain their relationship for now.

"It's a pleasure," Callum greeted, giving a shake as well.

"Same here," Lennox replied. "Lachlan tells me that you guys are very close."

"Oh yeah. We've been friends since we were wee lads."

Lennox gave me a pretty smirk and asked, "So, for almost five hundred years, then?"

Brodie's eyes widened and Callum asked (thankfully in a vampire whisper which Lennox couldn't hear), "*You've told him about your identity?*"

"*Just my age, and he thought I was joking.*"

Callum smiled at my mate and replied, "We certainly have a long history. Has Lach shown you the village already?"

"It's beautiful," he answered with a nod. "We're heading back to the field to play some football together."

"Aw, that sounds like fun," Brodie exclaimed.

Lennox tightened his grip on me as his nervousness rose. I understood why when he asked the pair, "Would you like to join us?" I was so proud of him for taking the step.

"Really?" Brodie asked. "I'd love to play! I never have though, so I probably won't be very good."

"I'd be happy to show you some things," Lennox offered, and both Brodie and Callum beamed.

"That's very nice of you," Callum replied with a bow of his head, as Brodie nodded happily. He added, *"He's a treasure,"* just for me; the moment Lennox showed Brodie kindness was the moment he won my friend's respect and favor. "How about I round up some more players and we have a proper game?"

I expected Lennox to get nervous again, but I only felt his excitement. "That sounds great."

"But let's tell them to meet us *after* Lennox gives me a lesson," Brodie requested, and Callum kissed his curly hair.

"Of course, m'anam. I can't wait to see your beautiful body on that field." His mate cuddled up with him while I felt yearning come from mine. Eager to meet his needs, I let go of his hand and slowly wrapped my arm around his waist, giving him the opportunity to stop me. But he only stepped closer, tucking himself into my side. The top of his head was level with the curve of my shoulder, and I felt like his protector.

"We'll see you at the field," I told my friends, and Callum winked before they took their leave. I chuckled when Freddie's jaws spread in a wide yawn. "I think he's ready

for a break. Let's get him home."

Chapter Five

Lennox

I couldn't believe the turn my life had taken. Just hours ago, I was homeless, helpless, and hungry. And now I was borderline snuggling with the most handsome man I'd ever seen in my life, on our way to the home he asked me to stay in, to get a ball so we could play my favorite game with people whom I hoped would be my friends.

I'm not sure what it was, but something about Brodie called to me; not in the way Lachlan called to me, which was that I wanted to get naked, sit on his lap, and kiss him until we couldn't breathe. Brodie spoke to me on a different level; his kindness and gentle nature (and I'll admit, his small size) made me feel like I could trust him.

Something told me that he'd understand what I'd been through, and wouldn't judge; that he'd only want to help. Maybe I was crazy for having those feelings after such a short meeting, but seeing him again made me excited, not scared. I was looking forward to seeing Callum again too; he was kind as well, and I knew how important he was to Lachlan.

Before I knew it, we were back at Lachlan's place, and he unfortunately took his arm from around my waist when we entered. Lachlan went down the hall and I smiled as I watched Freddie stretch out his back legs and yawn widely. He walked around in a circle several times before lying on the floor, resting his chin on his front paws. He had a belly full of bacon and had gotten lots of exercise outside, and I wouldn't be surprised if he spent the rest of the afternoon snoozing.

"Here we are," Lachlan announced when he stepped back into the living room carrying a football in one large hand. "Ready to hit the field?"

"Ready." I held out my hand hopefully, and Lachlan wasted no time in grasping it and linking our fingers together. It was a new experience for me, and I loved the way it felt. When this big, strong man held my hand so gently, I felt not only protected, but cherished; he could easily snap all of my bones if he wanted, but instead, he just softly stroked my knuckles as we walked.

I'm falling for this man. But it's so fast! I knew Malcolm for years and trusted him, and look how that turned out. But Lachlan is different; I know it. He had me alone and unconscious in his home and could have done anything to me, but he cared for me. He invited me to stay. Yeah, so did Malcolm...but then he attacked me with a syringe. A shudder rocked through me at the memory.

"Are you cold?" Lachlan asked me. "I can run back to the house to get you a jacket." We were nearly to the field already, which made his offer even sweeter.

"Naw, I'm okay, but thank you." He smiled and gave my hand a squeeze.

When we stepped onto the pitch, I saw Brodie and Callum waiting for us in the grass. Brodie waved excitedly over his head, and I did the same.

"The other guys will be here in half an hour," Brodie said after he and his husband jogged up to us. "So I'm ready to learn anything you can teach me before then."

Damn. Half an hour wasn't a long time to teach a whole sport. "Sure. What do you know about football?"

"I know you are supposed to kick the ball into the goal."

I smiled at him and replied, "Great; that's how you score points and is basically the whole idea of the game. Have you ever kicked a ball around, like in fitness class in school?"

Brodie's face dropped and he shook his head no. "I never had fitness class." Callum wrapped his arm around the man and kissed his head, and I worried I'd struck a nerve. I didn't understand what I said wrong, but I didn't want to make Brodie sad.

"That's okay, I'll teach you." Brodie's smile returned at my words and Lachlan handed me the ball before stepping back to give us some room. I looked at Callum and offered, "I can show you too if you like."

"Thank you, but I've played before. I'm happy to watch, though." He too stepped back, allowing Brodie and I plenty of space.

I dropped the ball to the ground and started our quick lesson. "Okay, so the first important thing is to never kick the ball with your toe; you won't be able to manage what direction it shoots off in. Kick it with this part of your foot." I lifted my leg and pointed to the insole of my trainer. "It will give you the most control."

Brodie nodded determinedly. "Got it."

"Okay, let's try passing it back and forth." I picked up the ball and jogged backwards several paces before dropping it again and kicking it to Brodie. When it rolled to a stop in front of him, he pulled his foot back and bumped the ball. It made it about halfway between us before stopping.

"I knew I'd be terrible," he sighed.

"No, no, no; that was great form," I encouraged. "Just try kicking it a little harder next time." He nodded and I grabbed the ball again. I went back to my starting position and sent the ball to him.

Brodie kicked it harder, alright; it left the ground completely and he gasped with worry when it soared towards me. Before the ball rammed into my stomach, I bounced it off of my knee and thumped it with my chest, sending it back to the ground in front of him.

Instead of kicking it back, Brodie ignored the ball as he clapped wildly. "That was incredible! I want to be on your team!" I laughed at his kind words, and Lachlan gave the broadest grin I'd seen yet, though it was pointed at me instead of Brodie.

Callum fake pouted as he put his hand on his chest. "I see how it is; you get a new friend and forget all about your poor, neglected husband." I got the feeling that they liked to joke around with each other, because Brodie just snorted and rolled his eyes.

"Of course I want to be on your team too; and Lach's." He motioned to all four of us and insisted, "This is the dream team right here." We all chuckled at the sweetheart before getting back to the lesson.

Before long, Brodie had the hang of passing the ball, and all four of us kicked it back and forth. When I taught him how to dribble down the field, however, he got tangled up a few times and tripped, falling to the ground. Each time, Callum was at his side in a blink, making sure he was okay. They were adorable, and I decided that if I was ever lucky enough to be in a relationship, I wanted it to be just like theirs; caring, silly, and sweet.

Just when Brodie (mostly) mastered dribbling, four more men appeared on the field. They were all built similar to Callum and Lachlan; tall, broad, and muscular. But that didn't mean that Brodie and I were at a disadvantage; sometimes being a smaller size was helpful in football because we could zip around the field more easily.

"Lennox, I'd like to introduce you to everyone," Callum announced. "This is Evan." He pointed to a large man with pretty, ice blue eyes. "He owns the glass shop here in town."

"Lach and I walked by your shop earlier when he was showing me the village," I told Evan. "Your work is beautiful."

"Thank you." He gave a proud grin and stuck his hand out for me to shake.

"I love it too," Brodie nodded. "Our house is full of his art because I can't get enough *and* because Callum spoils me." Callum grinned at his husband before giving him a swift kiss. They couldn't keep their hands off of each other, and it was lovely.

"And thanks for the invite," Evan added. "I haven't played for ages. I'm looking forward to it."

"Me too," the man beside him agreed. "I'm Lewis. I work as a waiter down at The Crown, and this is my mate Sean." They must have been close mates, because they were holding hands.

"It's nice to meet you both." I shook each of their hands before the last man spoke up.

"And my name is Kade. Welcome to our town. If there's *anything* you ever need, just let me know. I'll be happy to help in any way I can." Kade seemed nice, but also like a bit of a suck up. It looked like Lach and Brodie thought so too, with the way they were smirking at each other. Callum was watching Kade through slightly narrowed eyes.

Lachlan clapped his hands together. "Okay, let's get this game started. Lennox, Brodie, Callum and I are on a team, and the four of you will make up the other. Who wants to be the goal keepers?"

"I'll tend goal for our team," Callum offered.

"And I'll be happy to do it for our team," Kade insisted.

Lewis looked around and asked, "Where exactly *are* the goals?"

"I've got it covered." Callum reached into a deep pocket of his utility kilt and pulled out a can of spray paint. "I'll mark the field boundaries and goal boxes. It won't be as nice as nets, but I'll order some for our next game." It was generous of him to do so, and I hoped it meant we'd be playing often.

Once Callum had all of the lines sprayed onto the pitch, he tossed the empty paint can outside of the boundaries. We decided that the first team to three points would win, and Callum and Kade went to guard their goals. Sean and I faced one another on the center of the field with the ball between us.

We didn't have a referee, but we'd make do. Lewis pulled a coin from his pocket and said, "Lennox, call it," as he flicked it into the air.

"Heads," I chose, but when the coin was caught, Lewis announced that it was tails, so the other team got control of the ball first.

Since we had no ref or whistle, Lewis simply shouted, "Go!", and we were off.

Even though the men on the other team were large, they were graceful on the field. Their passes were fluid and they worked together perfectly. They quickly got the ball to the end of the pitch and Evan took a shot to the goal.

Luckily, Callum was talented too. He dove at the ball and caught it before it crossed the painted line of the goal. Brodie squealed and blew him kisses while he climbed back to his feet. After a lovestruck grin at his husband, Callum tossed the ball back in play, right towards me.

I chest bumped it again to slow it down and positioned it at my feet. I took off down the field, dribbling foot to foot. I heard someone at my heels and peeked over my shoulder to find Sean right behind me, so I passed the ball to Brodie, who was wide open.

He ran towards the goal too quickly and got his legs tied up. I barely had enough time to yell, "Watch your feet!" before he slipped on the ball, which shot out in front of him, and he took a faceplant to the ground.

I hurried to his side and helped him off of the grass just as everyone else surrounded him as well. It didn't matter what team they were on; everyone was friends here. I wiped a mud smear from Brodie's chin and asked worriedly, "Are you okay?" as Callum patted down his body to check for injuries.

"I'm great! Look!" He pointed behind me and when I turned around, I saw the ball sitting just inside the unattended goal box. "I made a goal! I scored the first point! Can you believe it?"

Callum cheered and lifted his husband high into the air, spinning him in a circle as Brodie laughed. "I'm so proud of you, m'anam!" We all congratulated Brodie and patted his back; even the guys he scored against. It was impossible not to be charmed by him.

"Our ball," Lewis announced once everyone settled down. He took it out of bounds and kicked it in, and the game was underway again.

We trudged back and forth across the field, passing, shooting, and groaning when we missed. Callum and Kade were both great goal keepers; they'd blocked nearly every shot taken against them. Though we played for what felt like (and very well could have been) hours, only three more goals had been made; one by Sean, one by Lewis, and one for our team by Lachlan.

The brisk air around me was the only thing keeping me from passing out in the grass; I was completely puggled. These other men had incredible endurance. Even Brodie seemed to be faring better than I was. With the score tied two-to-two, I called a timeout.

"What's up?" Brodie asked when he, Callum, and Lachlan huddled around me where I stood out of bounds. "Do we have a plan?"

"My first plan is to sit down for a minute," I admitted, and plopped my arse on the grass. I shrugged and flopped backwards, lying flat on the ground. I took deep breaths into burning lungs and joked, "My second plan is to inch my way back from death."

Lachlan was on his knees in an instant, patting my sweaty forehead dry. "I'm so sorry, little lamb; I wasn't thinking. Of course you need rest." He looked desperately up at Callum and said, "He also needs water." Callum nodded and ran towards town just as Brodie knelt on my other side and fanned my face.

"I'm okay, guys," I insisted with a breathy laugh. "I just need a second." They ignored me and continued to fawn all over me until Callum returned with a bottle of water. Lachlan propped me up and held the bottle to my lips so that I could drink, even when I insisted that I could do it myself. But I enjoyed his attention and care, so I didn't argue too much.

"How are you guys not even winded?" I asked them after I'd drained most of the bottle. Sure, they were in great shape, but they should have been showing *some* effects of working their bodies so hard. "I feel kind of pathetic right now."

The three of them shared uneasy looks before Lachlan smiled tightly. "You're *not* pathetic. Your body has been through a lot lately." Brodie's expression saddened, but he didn't ask any questions. Lachlan couldn't have answered them even if he had asked. But even though Lach wasn't sure of the details, his reasoning made sense; I'd put my body through some shite the past couple of weeks, so it wasn't a shock that my energy was low. "Just relax. Don't push yourself too hard; we'll call the game a tie."

I shook my head. "No, I want to finish."

Lachlan sighed before finally nodding his head. "Okay, but take your time. We'll start again when you feel up to it."

I rested a few more minutes, and ate a granola bar that Callum produced from his pocket. He must've brought it from wherever he got the water. He gave one to Brodie too, and once we were finished with the snack, I *did* feel much better, though it'd probably take a few days of meals and rest to feel totally like myself again.

"Okay," I said as I got to my feet, "Let's go kick some arse." My teammates chuckled and gave me high fives before everyone took our places on the field again. Or *I* did, anyway. I'm not sure what everyone else was doing because my attention was focused solely on Lachlan; somewhere between timeout and game play, he'd stripped off his t-shirt and was now standing on the field wearing only his black kilt and boots.

My jaw dropped as I stared and I couldn't close it if I wanted to; I was in complete awe of the sight before me. I knew Lachlan was strong by the way he carried me earlier and how he ran around this field like sex on legs, but I wasn't expecting his torso to be a sculpted display of thick, mounded muscles.

His abdomen, chest, and arms were all covered in black hair, and I wanted nothing more than to bury my face in it. I wanted to cuddle in bed and use him as my blanket. I wanted to see if he tasted as good as he looked.

Lachlan looked over at me and seemed to be breathing heavier than normal. At first I was worried that he was upset that I was blatantly checking him out, but his eyes trailed down my body too, and he didn't look disappointed. I wasn't sure how this sexy fucking bear could be interested in little ol' me, but I also wasn't about to complain.

When Lachlan's eyes met mine again, his face pinched up in panic. *Well, shite; I guess he isn't as interested as I thought.* But just then, I barely registered Brodie's call of, "Lenn, look out!"

I turned towards the sound just in time for the football to smash into my face. I wobbled on my feet for a moment before my arse found the ground again as stars danced before my eyes.

"Oh god, Lenn, I'm so sorry!" Brodie exclaimed as he rushed to my side and dropped to his knees. "Are you okay? I'm sorry; I didn't mean to. God, what is wrong with me? Why can't I stop hurting my friends' faces?"

I had no idea what he was talking about, and didn't have time to ask before Lachlan was at my other side, running his hands over my face and head to check for bumps. Before I could stop myself, I nuzzled my cheek into his palm and hummed, "Mm, that feels nice." His eyes widened a little before he smiled, and several of the other guys now standing around me gave good natured snickering.

"Oh good; you're flirting so you must be okay!" Brodie exclaimed before practically lying on top of me to give me a hug.

"Let's give him some air," Callum suggested as he peeled his husband off of me.

"Sorry; I just feel so bad."

I came to my senses, blushing as I pulled away from Lachlan's touch. "Don't feel bad," I told Brodie. "It was an accident; *I* was the one who wasn't paying attention. Besides, it's not a true game until someone gets clocked in the head with a rogue ball." More chuckles surrounded me, and then

Lewis offered me his hand and helped me off of the ground. "Let's try this again."

Everyone scattered to their places, except for Lachlan, who wrapped his arm around my shoulder and lowered his mouth to my ear. My pulse picked up when his breath fluttered across my skin as he asked, "I know you don't want to upset Brodie, but are you sure you're okay?"

I nodded and he let me loose. I smirked at him and said, "This is all your fault, you know; your body is too damn distracting." A smile slowly crossed his lips and my heart beat even faster. *Holy shite, I am* flirting! *And I think he's enjoying it!*

"Should I put my shirt back on?"

"Hell no."

Lachlan laughed loudly and deeply, and I thought for a moment that my legs would give out again. But somehow I managed to stay upright, even when he winked at me before hustling back to his spot. I stared at him for a few more moments before giving the game my attention again so that I wouldn't end up with a concussion.

Since the next goal determined the winner, game play was even more intense than before. Everyone pushed harder, ran faster, passed cleaner, and took every shot possible. But, Callum and Kade upped their game too; they dove at each shot that came their way, knocking them free of the goal.

Evan took possession of the ball and barrelled down the field towards Callum, who bent his knees and held out his hands as he readied to block the shot...but it never got that far. I zipped in front of Evan and kicked the ball right out from beneath his feet.

I was halfway down the field before the others realized what had happened. Footsteps thundered behind me, but I ran faster, keeping the ball close to my insoles so that no one could steal it.

Kade squatted low and stretched his fingers as I approached him. I planted my right foot on the ground and drew back my left, and Kade shuffled over to the left side of the goal. Once he was situated, I switched my feet and kicked the ball to the other side.

He made an impressive dive, but the ball scraped past his fingers and landed in the painted box.

Cheers erupted from behind me, the loudest coming from Lachlan. I turned around in time to see him running straight at me. He scooped me into his arms, and my legs instinctively wrapped around his waist. I cupped his cheeks and his excited shouting died away as we looked into one another's eyes.

I wanted to kiss him. I wanted to devour his lips and confess everything I was feeling for him. But I worried this wasn't the right moment; it wasn't private, and I didn't want everyone to overhear an intimate moment. I also didn't want them to witness my first attempt at a kiss in case it was terrible. So instead, I closed my eyes and pressed my forehead to his, hoping he understood what it meant.

"You did it!" Brodie's voice cut through the moment. "*We* did it!" When he hugged me from behind, Lachlan pulled back and smiled at me before gently placing me on the ground so that I could hug my new friend back properly.

Lachlan and Callum both joined in until we were a huddled mass of excitement. "You three were wonderful," Callum gushed.

"So were you," Brodie insisted as he broke from the group hug to cuddle up to his husband.

I nodded my agreement. "You and Kade are the best goal keepers I've ever seen." I turned to the rest of the group and insisted, "You *all* are the best players I've seen." We all exchanged high fives and back slaps as we congratulated each other on a great game. "I haven't had that much fun since...I can't even remember. I hope we can do it again."

"I'd love to play again," Evan replied with a wide grin. "You'll have to teach me how to steal the ball like that; that was slick."

"It's a deal." My heart pounded with happiness; these guys were accepting of me, and wanted to spend more time together, just as I did with them.

Evan's eyes turned to the sky and he said, "I think we're about to get some rain." I looked up at the clouds; they looked the same as they had all day.

"I think you're right," Callum agreed as he too looked upward. "We better get home before we get caught in it, m'anam."

Brodie nodded his agreement, but first, he wrapped me in one last hug. "I had so much fun today. Let's hang out again soon, okay?"

"Absolutely."

Brodie turned to his husband and held out his hands. "I'm awfully tired after that game." Callum snorted a laugh before hoisting Brodie into his arms, and his husband snuggled into his chest like it was something he'd done a thousand times before.

"It was a pleasure to meet you, Lennox," Callum smiled. "I'm sure we'll see each other again very soon."

"You bet," Lachlan agreed. Callum bowed his head and Brodie waved, and they took their leave.

Everyone else gave similar pleasantries and said their goodbyes before shuffling off as a group, with Lewis and Sean holding hands once more.

It looked like a great idea, so I picked up the football with one hand and gripped Lachlan's hand with the other. He smiled at me and gave it a squeeze before we walked off of the pitch. He stopped to pick his shirt up from the ground, threw it over his shoulder, and we strolled back towards town.

We only made it about halfway before the sky opened up and poured buckets of rain on us. I don't know how they sensed it, but Callum and Evan were right. Lachlan and I held tightly to each other as we laughed and sprinted back to his house.

When we burst through the front door, Freddie lifted his head long enough to see that it was just us before lying back down and continuing to snore.

"I'll put that back in the closet," Lach offered as he reached for the ball.

I handed it over before asking, "Would you mind if I took another shower? Or I can just dry myself off."

He sighed and rubbed his thumb across my hand again, which I was learning that I liked a *lot*. "Lennox, you can do whatever you want; I want you to be comfortable here. You don't have to ask for anything; have a snack, take a shower, grab a nap, watch TV...what's mine is yours."

It was too much, too generous, but I didn't know what to say except, "Thank you."

"I need to throw your clothes in the dryer, but I'll get you something of mine to wear for the evening."

I huffed a laugh and said, "I think all of your things will be way too big for me."

"Would you like me to call Brodie again?"

"No, I don't want him to get out in this rain. I don't mind wearing something of yours." Honestly, I was ecstatic about the idea of having his clothing on my body. "I just hope you don't think I look silly."

"Trust me, little lamb; that's not possible." I ducked my head, wondering if I'd ever get used to hearing his sweet words, and hoping that he never stopped saying them. "I'll put them on the bathroom sink again."

"Thank you. But you can take a shower first if you want." *If you want.* I felt like a dobber as I said it; it was his house, of course he could.

"I've got two bathrooms," he shrugged, "So I'll jump in the other one once I lay out your clothes."

I nodded and hurried off to the bathroom I used earlier, not wanting to drip on his floor any more than I already had. I stripped off my sopping wet clothes and stepped into a hot shower.

The water felt incredible; it washed away the sweat and rain from my skin, and the heat relaxed my sore muscles. Just as I grabbed a bottle of body wash, I heard the door slowly creak open before shutting again almost immediately. I trusted Lachlan not to enter without permission.

I trust Lachlan. There I was, totally naked and completely vulnerable, but I wasn't worried about what may happen. I didn't think I could trust anyone after what happened with Malcolm - at least not so soon - but with Lachlan, it came naturally.

The more time I spent with him, the happier I became. I felt more like myself; more like the guy who enjoyed making people laugh and being with friends. I liked who I was when I was with Lachlan.

I smiled as I squirted some soap onto a washcloth and gave it a sniff. I loved his soap; it smelled crisp and sporty, but strangely, not like Lachlan himself. He smelled like a delicious mix of mint and lavender; it relaxed me every time I detected it on his skin.

Once I was clean and rinsed, I turned off the water and dried myself with one of his thick, fluffy towels. They were so much nicer than the scratchy ones at St. Joseph's. I dried my hair the best I could before combing my fingers through it. Lach probably had an actual comb in one of the drawers beneath the sink, but I didn't want to search through his personal things.

I pulled on the plain white t-shirt that Lach chose for me, and snorted when I saw that it nearly reached my knees. Not only was he a head taller than me, but he was also *much* thicker, so the fabric hung loose on my thin body.

I stepped into the pair of gray sleep shorts Lach left for me, but when I settled them on my hips, they immediately dropped to the floor. *Oh my.* They didn't have a drawstring; just an elastic waistband, so I had no way to make them smaller. Lachlan didn't lay out any underwear, so all I had to cover myself was the thin cotton t-shirt.

I folded the shorts and put them back on the sink before stepping out of the bathroom. I cupped my hands over my groin and tiptoed down the hall. I heard noise in the kitchen, so I peeked my head around the corner to find Lachlan messing with something on the stovetop, while dressed only in a pair of sweatpants. *God dammit. Why does he have to be so sexy when I have nothing to hold back my dick?*

Lach looked over his shoulder and saw my face peeking out from behind the wall. "Hey there; is something wrong?"

"Erm, would you happen to have any smaller pants?"

"I'm sorry, but I gave you the smallest ones I have."

Damn. "Well, would you be upset if I didn't wear any?" A spoon slipped from Lachlan's hand and clattered to the floor. "I'm covered," I added quickly. "The shirt is long enough, but if it bothers you, I can wrap a towel around my waist."

"I don't-" Lachlan paused to clear his throat when his voice sounded raspy. "I don't mind." He bent to pick up his spoon, only to drop it a second time when I stepped into the room. "Oh, wow." My cheeks flushed as I shuffled over to a barstool and took a seat. "I'm sorry; I just...*really* like seeing you in my clothes."

"I really like wearing them," I admitted, though I kept to myself that what I liked most was that *he* wasn't wearing much. "What are you making?"

"Huh?" I pointed to the stovetop behind him and Lach shook his head. "Oh, right. I'm heating up some beef stew for dinner. I just made it yesterday." He tossed the floor spoon in the sink and grabbed another one from a drawer. "Is that okay? It's nothing fancy, but it's good comfort food on a rainy evening."

"It sounds delicious, and I never need anything fancy."

"Plus I still have some butter tablet for dessert."

I raised a hand and announced, "I'm sold," making him chuckle.

"I was thinking; would you want to come to the bakery with me tomorrow? You're welcome to stay here if you like, but I thought you might want to join me and sample all of the goodies I make."

"You had me at 'sample all of the goodies'." I smiled when he laughed again; I loved the deep, rich sound. "I'd love to come with you. And if it's okay, I'd like to help you bake, too. I love eating sweeties, but I've always wanted to learn how to make them."

Lachlan surprised me by reaching across the countertop to take my hand. "You don't know what that means to me. I'd love to teach you." He kissed my knuckles and left me breathless when he turned away again to grab a stack of four bowls from the cupboard. He filled three with stew and one with water and my heart warmed over his care for Freddie. As if he heard my thoughts, Lachlan said, "Tomorrow we can pick up some dog food."

"If I were Freddie, I'd rather keep eating your cooking."

He thanked me with a wide smile before asking, "Would you like to watch a movie while we eat?"

"Sure." I grabbed the two bowls for Freddie and made my way into the living room, blushing at Lachlan's soft moan as he walked behind me.

We settled onto the sofa next to each other while Freddie ate happily on the floor. We decided on a science fiction flick (my favorite) and tucked into our meals as well. The stew was delicious, as was the tablet we devoured afterwards.

But the best part was the feeling of contentment and belonging that filled me; Lachlan tucked me under his arm as we watched the movie, and Freddie jumped onto the sofa to lay at my side. I brushed my fingers through his scruffy fur and couldn't help thinking this was the perfect way to spend every evening. I was happy and at peace.

I knew I needed to have a conversation with Lachlan, but even that didn't worry me. I was ready. Once the movie ended, I'd tell him everything. Until then, I rested my head on his chest, breathed in his soothing scent and smiled.

*****

I jerked awake at the sound of thunder shaking glass. I blinked my eyes, trying to adjust them to the darkness as I looked around; I was in a bedroom, tucked beneath thick blankets, alone except for Freddie, who was curled up at my feet.

I must have fallen asleep during the movie and Lachlan brought me in here. I was normally a light sleeper, but I'd been so comfortable with him and so tired, it wasn't hard to see how I didn't stir when he carried me in.

I flinched again when lightning cracked outside the window to my left. I clenched the covers in fists when thunder boomed and sheets of rain pelted the glass. I hated storms. The longer I listened to the ruckus outside, the further my newfound peace scattered away, and old anxieties and fears crept in.

There was only one thing; one *person* who could make me feel safe again. I hated to bother Lachlan, but I needed him. I needed his protective hold and the comfort I felt with him. The more I thought of him, the greater the desire to be with him grew until my chest actually ached. I scooped Freddie into my arms and entered the hallway to look for Lachlan's room, silently praying that he let me in.

Chapter Six

Lachlan

I stared at the ceiling of my bedroom and smiled as I replayed the memories of my day with Lennox; from caring for his basic needs, to seeing his sporty, fun side, to tucking him into bed. He looked so sweet when he fell asleep on my chest, after he only made it halfway through the movie.

As much as I wanted to wake him up and spend more time with him, I knew his body was exhausted. So, I carefully took him in my arms and carried him to my guest bedroom. Obviously I wanted him with me, but I didn't want to overstep his boundaries.

I lay him gently on the mattress and tucked the blanket around his slim frame to make sure he'd be warm enough. And then the greatest thing happened; Lennox whispered my name in his sleep, and a tiny smile pulled at his lips. My mate was dreaming of me, and that precious moment would live in my memory forever.

I sat upright when I heard shuffling coming from the hallway. I immediately worried that something was wrong with Lennox, but before I could even swing a leg out of my bed, his pretty face appeared in the crack of my open door.

"I'm sorry; did I wake you up?" he asked nervously.

"No, I was already awake. Is something wrong?"

He chewed on his lip as he stepped further into my room. "It's...it's Freddie. He's afraid of the storm."

I looked at the pup in his arms; Freddie was snoozing soundly without a care in the world. Lennox, however, appeared nervous and his fear and shame ballooned into the room. I wanted to give him comfort without embarrassing him further, so I asked, "Would he feel better if he slept in here?"

Lennox nodded and placed Freddie at the foot of my bed, but of course that didn't solve the problem. If anything, my mate's anxiety only rose after he gave up his companion, so I suggested, "Maybe Freddie would be more comfortable if we were *both* with him," as I pulled down the blanket in invitation.

Lennox practically ran around the bed and climbed in beside me. Without saying a word, he pulled the covers up to his chin and scooted close to my side, resting his head on my shoulder. I pushed love and comfort into him, and his fear flitted away.

I thought that Lennox would fall asleep again quickly, but instead he took me by surprise when he said quietly, "I lost my parents in a storm like this."

The unexpected news broke my heart. Wanting to give him any comfort I could, I wrapped him tightly in my arms. "I'm so sorry, little lamb."

"It was four years ago. We were going home after eating dinner at a restaurant. The rain picked up out of nowhere and got so strong that we couldn't see out of the windows. My da was driving and he wanted to be safe, so he pulled onto the side of the road, put his hazard lights on, and said we'd listen to the radio until the weather calmed down."

He took a deep, shaky breath before continuing, "We were singing along to a song, even dancing in our seats and being silly. We thought we were safe there; Da thought he was doing the right thing."

I caressed my hand up and down his arm. "What happened?"

"A driver on the opposite side of the road was going too fast. Their car hydroplaned in standing water and slid across the street. It hit our car head on. It jarred me a bit, but I wasn't hurt. But my parents..."

When he didn't continue, I offered, "I'm so sorry," again. I wasn't sure what else to say; I couldn't imagine the pain and anguish he felt when he watched his parents pass at such a young age.

"I think about the accident every time it storms. I remember everything and I get scared and upset. I know it's dumb; it was so long ago and I'm a grown man now. I shouldn't be feeling this way, but-"

"Lennox, listen to me," I requested gently. "Nothing you're feeling is dumb. It doesn't matter how old you are or how long it's been; you went through a terrible tragedy. My heart aches for you and the pain you've endured, and I think you're so strong to have made it through this. Please never hide your feelings from me; I will never judge you, and I want to help you. Being scared or sad doesn't make you weak; it makes you human, and you have the most beautiful soul I've ever known."

Lennox nuzzled his cheek against my shoulder as he sniffed. "Thank you. I'm sorry

I didn't tell you sooner, and I'm sorry I lied about Freddie being scared."

I smiled and rested my head on his. "It's okay, little lamb. I'm honored that you felt safe enough to tell me." But one thing worried me greatly. "Have you been on your own the past four years?"

Lennox shook his head no before bursting into tears. I held him tightly as he dove into his heart wrenching story of courts, a boy's home, and the pain caused by a man who was supposed to offer his help and guidance. I wanted Malcolm's head. I was proud of Lennox for fighting him off and getting away, but the 'doctor' (he didn't deserve the title) got off *way* too easily. He tried to do unspeakable things to my mate and if I ever laid eyes on him, I'd make him pay in unspeakable ways.

"And I know you're not like Malcolm," Lennox sniffled, "But when we met, I was scared and that's why I hid so much from you and I'm sorry. But now I'm afraid of what you think of me. You know I'm a thief; I stole Freddie and I tried to steal from you. I would've stolen from anyone to eat. Everything I own is in my backpack, and it isn't much. I'm scared you'll see how pathetic I am and not want me around anymore."

"But I don't want to leave you. I've been nervous and depressed for so long, but you make me happy. You make me feel truly safe for the first time in years. I trust you and I want to stay with you even though it's selfish and I have nothing to give you. I'm afraid you won't want me now that you know what a basket case I am, but I need you because I...I think I'm falling in love with you."

My brain spun, trying to track the plethora of emotions he stirred within me. Lennox pulled on my heartstrings in every possible way. I scooted down the mattress until we were eye level with one another; I wanted him to see my sincerity when I spoke.

"Lennox, you are not a thief; you're Freddie's savior, and you're a survivor. You're also stronger and braver than you know; not only for enduring what you've been through, but for opening up and trusting someone after you've been hurt. I told you when I invited you to stay that I just wanted to help, but I also want to *be* with you. I don't care about your material belongings because you've given me the most precious gift; your beautiful heart, and it's more than I deserve."

I cupped his smooth cheek in my palm and dried the tears from his skin. "I promise to never betray your trust. I swear I will protect you. I want you here, and I *need* you here because I love you too."

Lennox's lips trembled and his eyes danced with moisture as he whispered, "I really want you to kiss me right now."

He didn't have to tell me twice; I'd been waiting for this moment since we met. My heart pounded as I leaned in close, and it skipped a beat when our lips touched.

I kissed him tenderly and slowly, relishing the feel of his plush lips against mine. My hand slid to the back of his head, where I carded my fingers through his soft hair. He was fragile yet so strong, hidden, but brave; a paradox I'd happily explore for all of my days.

Knowing it was his first kiss, I moved ever so slowly as I extended my tongue and ran it along Lennox's plump bottom lip. He hummed softly, vibrating my flesh before opening up to my exploration. I slid my tongue along his, tasting the buttery sweetness that clung to his skin. I lapped against him and tickled the roof of his mouth, and then Lennox took me by surprise.

He crammed his tongue into my mouth and licked wildly at every surface. He gripped the back of my head and pulled me closer until our teeth bumped together. Lennox devoured my lips until his saliva dripped down my chin. It was slippery and sloppy and absolutely wonderful.

With every nip of his teeth or slide of his tongue, my heart beat faster and I pulled his body closer. Fire flowed through my veins and my flesh burned with need. Lennox's thigh barely brushed against my stone hard cock and a low growl rumbled in my chest.

Lennox pulled his swollen, wet lips from mine and looked at me with dark but rounded eyes. "Was that a good growl or a bad growl?" He was sexy as sin but still sweet as an angel.

"So good," I answered in a raspy voice, and he sighed in relief.

But then his apprehension clouded the air as he chewed his lip, drawing every ounce of my attention. "Lach, I want more with you, but I honestly don't know what the hell I'm doing. I've only ever touched...you know...myself, and I don't want to do anything wrong or-"

I stopped his words with a firm kiss, not only to lessen his worries, but also, if I were to listen any more about him touching himself, I was going to embarrass *myself* in my sleep pants.

When our lips parted, I wrapped an arm around his waist and hauled his body on top of mine until he straddled my hips. "Give me your hands, little lamb." He did as I asked and I placed a kiss to each of his palms before settling them on my bare chest.

"I want you to do whatever feels right; touch, tease, taste, and explore all you want. Nothing that you desire is wrong; my body is all yours, and everything you do to me feels incredible."

He gifted me with a beautiful smile. "I really do love you, you know that?" I smiled back as I nodded. "You take all of my worries away." It was everything I wanted for him; to know that he was safe with me in every way.

Lennox's gaze dropped to my chest as he slowly caressed his fingers through the hair on my pecs. I moaned when he brushed over my nipple, and his smile turned naughty.

I moaned again when he tweaked my other nipple, pinching it until it contracted into a hard point before moving his hands back into the patch of hair over my sternum. I thought he was wanting another kiss when he leaned down, but he said, "I've wanted to do this all day," before burying his face into my hairy chest.

"This is so nice," he said in a muffled voice as he nuzzled against me. "I want to feel it everywhere." He whipped the shirt he wore over his head and plastered his body onto mine. His skin was like silk on mine and as incredible as it felt to have the weight of his warm, naked body pressing down on me, his hard cock lying on my stomach, I needed to see him.

I didn't want to rush him, but the desire to lay eyes on his beautiful body was too great to resist. I kissed the top of his head and whispered into his hair, "Please, may I see you?"

Lennox's breathing picked up against my chest while his anticipation swirled with his nervousness. He propped his hands on my chest and pushed until he sat upright, and I moaned at the sight of his gorgeous bare body.

I trailed my gaze down his creamy skin, loving his pale pink nipples and the tight smoothness of his abdomen. My heart pounded as I looked lower, to a patch of cropped blond hair covering his groin and his balls, which rested on my stomach. Lennox's hard cock was slim, cut, and about six inches long.

"Lennox, you are so beautiful," I whispered in awe.

"So are you." He trailed his hand down my stomach but kept his eyes on mine. "Can I see the rest of your body?"

"I told you, little lamb; it's yours."

Lennox shifted himself so that he rested on his knees beside me. His hands trembled as he curled his fingers around the waistband of my sleep pants and slowly pulled them down my legs.

His breath caught when he uncovered the tip of my firm cock, and his eyes widened as he slid the fabric down, unveiling every thick inch. He licked his lips at the sight of my hairy, heavy balls, and quickly pulled my pants the rest of the way down my legs and off of my feet.

"Good lord." Lennox straddled my knees and pressed his shaking hands to my thighs. He slowly trailed them up and cupped my sack in his palm. His fingers caressed my sensitive skin and I hummed when he gently squeezed. "Does that feel good?"

"Oh Lennox, it feels incredible." He squeezed, massaged, and bounced my orbs in his palm until my chest swelled with heavy breaths, but I still felt his trepidation in his touch and the air around us. "Don't hold back," I begged breathlessly.

Lennox bit his lip in determination before scooting upward and pushing his hips forward until our balls touched. He enveloped both of our fuzzy sacks in his hand and kneaded our flesh together. Our balls rolled and bumped together as I moaned and goosebumps popped up on my arms.

Lennox moved his hand to the base of his cock and pressed his tip to my shaft. Our heated flesh brushed together as he traced my length, painting my skin with clear, sticky fluid. I'd never experienced anything like this, and it was beautiful to watch him explore my body in his own way.

He touched his slippery tip to mine, rubbing against me in slow circles. My breath caught when a large drip trickled from his slit and balanced over mine, and I moaned low and deep when he slid our heads against one another.

Lennox pressed the underside of his shaft to mine; my cock was a couple of inches longer and a good bit thicker than his own, and they looked perfect together. Lennox wrapped his fingers around both of us and gave a slow tug.

"You feel so good against me," Lennox moaned as he stroked us again. "Your cock is so thick and warm." I only managed a throaty moan in reply; I didn't expect the sexy words from my mate, and they took my breath away. "Damn, this is amazing."

Lennox trapped his plump bottom lip between his teeth and stroked us a little faster. His brows tucked closer together, but he kept his eyes open and trained on me.

I growled, "You're so fucking beautiful," and Lennox gave a whimper so sweet and so sultry that my body acted on its own accord; my hand folded around his, squeezing firmly as I jacked us.

"Oh, Lach," Lennox groaned as his breathing picked up. His eyes pinched shut, but I couldn't take mine off of his body. His slim chest swelled as he moaned and whispered my name. His jaw went slack as he sucked air in through his plush lips, and his wild hair bounced against his forehead.

His hand trembled beneath mine as I pumped us faster. Pre-cum dripped from both of us onto my stomach, and my mouth watered when our combined scent hit my nostrils.

"Oh, Lach!" he repeated as I stroked us faster. His eyes popped open and looked at me with pure need. "Lach, I'm gonna come!"

"Yes," I pleaded, jerking our cocks furiously even when his hand went still, "Don't hold back, Lennox; come for me!"

His head fell back onto his shoulders and he cried out as his whole body lurched forward. His dick pulsed in my hand and against my aching shaft before a stream of cum burst from him onto my stomach.

Lennox moaned and trembled as I continued to pump his sensitive flesh. I breathed deeply, inhaling his sweet scent as his whimpers kissed my ears. My balls rolled and pulled towards my body as pressure ballooned in my pelvis.

I grunted Lennox's name through clenched teeth as my cock jumped in my hold. Thick white gobs erupted from me, splattering over my mate's seed.

I barely got my hand unwrapped from his when Lennox collapsed on top of me, squishing our spunk between us. He captured my lips with his, giving me more sloppy, wonderful kisses.

"That was incredible," Lennox whispered when he broke our kiss. "I always wondered what it would be like, but I never imagined it would be so..." He shrugged his shoulders. "The only word I can think of is incredible."

"It was, and so are you," I told him as I combed his locks off of his forehead. "And just think; we have so much more to discover together."

His lips spread into a shy smile. "I wouldn't want to discover them with anyone else. I'm so blessed that you found me."

My heart warmed at his precious words. "I feel the same way. I've been searching for you my whole life, little lamb."

We parted only long enough for me to wipe our skin clean with Lennox's discarded shirt, and then we snuggled naked beneath the blankets, with our legs tangled together and my mate using my chest as a pillow. I peeked down at the pup at our feet, having completely forgotten he was there, but he was still snoozing soundly and unbothered by our movement or noise.

I kissed Lennox's head and caressed my hand up and down his back. The storm still raged outside, but I only felt peace and happiness coming from him. I was happy to be a source of strength and comfort for him, no matter the situation.

"Sleep well," I whispered into his hair, and Lennox nuzzled his cheek against my skin.

"You too. Love you." My heart pounded at the words I'd waited half a millennium to hear, yet admittedly wondered if they'd ever come. Hearing them from my sweet Lennox's lips was worth the wait.

"And I love you." Within moments, my mate was sound asleep, and I followed shortly after with a smile on my face.

Chapter Seven

Lachlan

Lennox stirred in my arms, stretching with a groan before he smiled up at me.

"Mornin', beautiful," I greeted him before kissing his forehead. "How did you sleep?" I was awake most of the night, listening to his steady breathing and caressing his smooth skin; he seemed to sleep like a rock, but I wanted to make sure he rested well.

"That was the best sleep I've had in years." He stroked my chest and added, "I think it was this comfy pillow." Lennox smiled wider when I chuckled and my chest vibrated beneath his fingers. "I *was* hoping I'd wake up before you, though."

"Why's that?"

"Well, you made me breakfast yesterday, so I was going to return the favor. I wanted to bring you breakfast in bed, but I slept too long."

My heart skipped a beat at his sweetness. "I don't know what I did to deserve someone so great, but you never have to do any favors for me."

"I wouldn't call it a *favor*; I can't cook like you can, so it probably would've just been toast or something, but I wanted to do something special for you."

I was grateful for him and anything he did for me, so I told him with a shrug, "I love toast," and he gave me a pretty smile. Lennox would probably never wake up before me since I slept so little, but now that I knew this was important to him, I'd definitely fake sleeping in every now and then. But for today, "Why don't we make breakfast together? We can go on to the bakery and start making things for the shop, but also make a special treat for us."

"Have I mentioned that I love you?" I laughed again - it was impossible not to when he made me so happy.

Freddie stood up at the end of the bed and stretched as he gave a big yawn. He trotted up to Lennox and nudged his hand with his snout until my mate pet his head.

"Good morning, buddy. Do you need to go outside?" Freddie's ears perked up at the word and his tail whipped back and forth. "Okay, let me get some clothes on and I'll take you out."

I moaned aloud when Lennox stood up and I got an eyeful of his cute little round arse, and Lennox ducked his head as he giggled. If I didn't know Freddie was about to pop, I would've hauled my mate back into bed to love on him. But, I let him go so he could retrieve an outfit. It was a damn shame to cover up his beautiful body, but I sure as hell didn't want the neighbors to get a peek.

I got dressed as well, in a gray kilt, a navy blue t-shirt, and my black boots. While Lennox and Freddie were outside, I heated up the last bit of beef stew for the pup's breakfast. After the bakery closed, I'd buy a bag of dog food. I didn't mind cooking for him, but I wanted to make sure he got the right nutrition.

"All set," Lennox announced when the two of them re-entered the house. My mate looked adorable as always in a pair of jeans, a red long sleeve tee, and his black knit cap. He watched with a smile as Freddie ran to his food and ate greedily, and then he slung his arms around my waist. "Thank you for taking such good care of him; of both of us."

"It's my pleasure, little lamb." I kissed the top of his head and told him, "Let's go get our breakfast too."

The sun rose above the surrounding hilltops as we walked hand in hand to the bakery. Ordinarily, I went in hours earlier to begin baking, but after Lennox's emotional night, I wanted him to get plenty of rest. Not a single vampire here could fault me for looking after my mate.

"This place is so cute," Lennox complimented when we walked inside and he looked around at the fireplace and quaint tables in the dining area. I tossed a couple of logs into the hearth and had a flame going within minutes. When I stood, my mate was giving me a curious look.

"What's on your mind?"

He tapped his chin as he looked up and down my body. "You have this cute little bakery where you make sweeties, but you can start a fire like you're flipping on a light switch, carry me around like I'm a feather, and you look like a soldier."

"I *was* a warrior once upon a time," I admitted, and Lennox's jaw dropped.

"Really?" At my nod, he asked, "Will you tell me about it? I mean, unless it's too sad or scary."

I smiled at his sweetness and leaned down to touch my forehead to his. "I want to tell you everything." Not just about my past, but about my identity and our bond. I'd taken things slow because of his apprehension, but now that I had his trust and his love, it was time. "But let's get breakfast started first." Everything was easier to talk about over food.

Lennox nodded and followed me into the kitchen, where he pointed at the large wood burning oven in the corner. "Is this what you bake with?"

"Aye. It's what I was taught on, and what I prefer to use," I explained as I stoked flames within it.

"Who taught you to cook?"

I smiled as I stood upright. "My da taught me everything I know. And my ma *loved* that she had two bakers in the house."

"That's so sweet. My ma was the baker in our house; she was the one who got me hooked on sweeties since hers were so delicious. I never learned from her, though; I wish I had." Instead of appearing saddened, Lennox smiled. "I'm excited to learn from you."

I stole a kiss and told him, "Many people have asked me through the years why I work alone instead of hiring an assistant. Part of the reason is just that I enjoy the work, and can manage on my own, but also, I see baking as an intimate experience; sharing recipes and memories that I've held close to my heart is a very special act, and I only wanted to share it with a very special person."

Love and happiness rolled off of Lennox as his eyes went glassy. "And I'm that person?"

"Of course you are. Lennox, I've never been in love before, but when I saw you for the first time, I knew it was Fate; I'd met the man I wanted to spend my life with. You and Freddie are my family now. I want to share everything with you."

I rocked back onto my heels when Lennox slammed into me, wrapping his arms around my thick waist. He lurched up on his toes, puckering his lips, so I leaned down and kissed him deeply. Our tongues tangled and our hands gripped; I was content to kiss him all day long, until his stomach gave an angry growl.

I pulled away and smiled at the way his eyelids fluttered open. "I think we better get back to baking." Lennox nodded and I pulled open the doors to my large refrigerator, revealing several baking sheets covered in blobs of dough.

"What are those?"

"These are scones; or they *will* be once we bake them. I like to make dough beforehand and refrigerate it. It makes things easier in the mornings and they hold their shapes better this way."

"Smart. What flavors are there?"

"These two pans are cranberry-orange, these are blueberry, and these last two are cinnamon."

"They all sound delicious," he remarked before licking his lips.

"You're welcome to any of them, but we still need to make our special dish." I slid the sheets onto the stone racks above the fire and turned to Lennox. "How do you feel about Empire biscuits?"

"They're one of my favorites."

"Brilliant." They were fairly simple to make and didn't take long in the oven. "Could you please grab the sugar, flour, and confectioners' sugar while I get the ingredients from the refrigerator?"

"Sure!" Lennox jogged to the shelves on the back wall with an excited grin as I retrieved the butter, raspberry preserves, milk, and maraschino cherries. We met back at the large wooden table in the center of the room.

"Okay, the first thing we need to do is chop up this butter," I told him as I handed over a large block.

"All of it?"

"Aye."

"Damn, that's a lot of butter."

"That's why the biscuits are so good," I shrugged, and Lennox enthusiastically nodded his agreement. While he cut the block, I measured sugar into a mixing bowl.

"Nicely done," I complimented when he had the butter chopped into nearly matching squares, and he beamed from ear to ear. "Put them in the bowl and we'll cream them together." I got an electric mixer off of the shelf since it'd be tough to mix by hand. Ordinarily I'd give the butter time to soften, but I was trying to hurry things along to feed my mate.

"Okay, just hold it like this," I instructed with the mixer, "And keep it in the bowl or else you'll have batter splatter on your shirt."

Lennox snorted as he took the mixer. "Batter splatter."

I chuckled and stood behind him. Lennox placed the beaters in the bowl and turned it on full speed, and the mixer nearly flew out of his grip. I covered his hand with my own and decreased the speed before guiding him by easing the mixer around. "There you go."

I lowered my head to the nape of his neck and deeply breathed in his scent; it was sweeter than anything in the kitchen. I pressed gentle kisses along his hairline and onto the side of his throat. His pulse vibrated against my lips, causing my fangs to stretch and tingle. I hadn't fed in three days, and my body craved my mate's blood. My throat tightened and ached with thirst.

"I can see why cooking is intimate," Lennox said, backing his arse into my thighs. After one last peck to his throat, I forced my attention back to the food. If I focused on the luscious blood in his veins, my body would continue to prepare for claiming, and I didn't want to frighten him.

I cleared the tightness from my throat and lifted the bag of flour from the table. "For the next part, would you rather sift or stir?"

"I'll try sifting."

I measured and piled flour into the sifter and held it above the bowl of batter. "Turn this handle nice and slow and I'll stir it together."

"Got it." Lennox cranked the handle, watching as the white powder fell over the butter mixture. "Why do we have to sift it?" I liked that he was asking questions; I wanted to teach him everything I knew.

"It gets rid of any clumps in the flour; that way our biscuits won't be too dense."

I smiled when he replied, "Interesting," and it stretched wider at the way he tucked his lip between his teeth in concentration as he slowly turned the knob. "That's all of it," he announced when the last of the powder landed in the bowl.

He beamed with pride when I told him, "Great job." After a few more stirs, I said, "Okay, see how we've got nice, thick dough now?" He nodded. "We need to roll it out flat so we can cut it into circles. Will you sprinkle a little flour onto the table so that it doesn't stick?"

"Sure!" Lennox dumped a mountain of flour onto the tabletop and spread his hand through it until white padding covered nearly all of the wood. "Is that enough?"

I had to bite my cheek to keep from chuckling; he was so damn adorable and excited (and maybe a little overzealous), and I loved it all. "That's perfect. You're a natural at this, little lamb." I thought his face was going to crack with how brightly he smiled.

I plopped the ball of dough onto the flour carpeting and retrieved a rolling pin. "Now we just need a little flour on this-" I bit my cheek again when Lennox scooped two handfuls onto the pin - "Lovely. So, you're going to hold these two handles and roll the dough out nice and smooth. We need it about this thick." I held my thumb and first finger apart to demonstrate.

Lennox nodded and pressed the pin to the dough. He pushed until he grunted, but the roller didn't move. He repositioned and pushed again, but still had no luck. He looked back at me and sighed. "This is tougher than I thought it would be."

"It can be a little tricky to get started, but I'll help you." I stood behind him and covered his hands with mine. "So instead of pushing straight down, we're going to rock it back and forth." I guided his hands forward and back until we made a flat spot in the dough. "There we go." Our bodies rocked together as we pushed and pulled. My skin burned with need as it brushed against his, and my heart pounded at the way he was tucked into my hold as I helped guide him.

"Hey Lach?" I hummed in question and Lennox added, "I love baking with you." Whether it was because he felt the heat between us or he was just enjoying the lesson, it didn't matter; my feelings were the same. I'd waited so long for this moment, and it was better than I ever pictured.

"So do I." I kissed his neck again and his hands jerked forward, pulling the dough until a crack formed down the center.

"Oh no, I tore it!"

"It's okay." I let loose of his hand to pinch the crack closed. "That's the great thing about dough; it's easy to fix." He sighed in relief and I kissed him again. "I think we're ready to cut the shapes." I fetched two cutters from a shelf and held them out for Lennox to inspect; one was a plain circle and the other had scalloped edges. "Which one would you like to use?"

"I think we should go fancy," he decided, pointing to the scalloped cutter. I winked at him and put the plain circle back on the shelf.

"Good choice. If you want to begin cutting, I'll prepare the baking sheets."

"On it," he replied with a thumbs up. I loved how seriously he was taking his tasks, and that he was enjoying this as much as I was.

As I covered several baking pans with parchment paper, Lennox got to work on the biscuit shapes. I smiled when he mumbled,

"Shite, I messed that one up," before calming himself with, "It's okay; they're easy to fix," and pinching the shape back together.

I propped my elbow on the table and rested my chin in my hand, watching him as he worked. He rotated between gnawing on his bottom lip and peeking the tip of his tongue out of the corner of his mouth when he concentrated. He was so damn beautiful.

"Aaand done," Lennox announced when he cut the last circle. "How do they look?"

"Perfect." The ones with tiny rips or pinch marks were the best of all. We transferred the circles onto the baking sheets and I slid them into the oven along with the scones, which still had some baking time left. The biscuits would only take about ten minutes.

I finished wiping the tabletop clean when I noticed Lennox eyeing me curiously. "I know Freddie and I are your family-" my heart swelled at how easily he accepted it as fact, "But do you have any others? Are your ma and da...I mean, are they still...?" He didn't finish his question, but I understood what he was trying to ask.

"Aye, they are, although they don't live *here*; they moved to Spain many years ago since they have lots of friends and loved ones there. We're still close, though; we visit each other once every ten years or so."

"Ten *years*?" Lennox asked in surprise. I understood why it sounded like a long time to him, but in the scheme of eternity, a deKade was nothing.

"I also have two brothers; the oldest is named Alister, and then there's Bruce. I'm the baby of the family."

"Do your brothers live close by?"

"Bruce moved to Spain with my parents, and he lives there with his wife and daughters, who are grown. Alister lives in Wales; his wife's family is from there."

"Have you ever visited Spain?" I nodded; I'd been there many times. "What's it like?"

"It's beautiful there; it has stunning beaches and gardens, and gorgeous architecture. My favorite thing to do when I visit is to tour old castles."

"I'd love to see a castle one day," Lennox answered with a sparkle in his eye.

"Then I will take you."

"Really?" His hope and excitement swirled in the air.

"Really." I cupped his cheek and ran my thumb along his smooth skin. "I want to show you everything in this world." I'd do anything for the pretty smile he gave me. "Where else would you like to visit?"

Lennox thought for a moment before answering, "I've always wanted to see

America; the Statue of Liberty, Mount Rushmore, the Redwoods...I read about all of those places in school, but I'd love to see them for myself."

"Then we will visit them as well." I sealed my promise with a kiss to his forehead. "You know, I have very good friends who live in America. They're actually coming for a visit very soon. My old friends Flynn and Fletcher moved to the states after they married their husband, but they've been a little homesick and-"

"I'm sorry to interrupt, but did you say their *husband*? As in one guy?"

I nodded. "They are both married to a man named Sam. Oh, and Flynn and Fletcher are twin brothers." Lennox blinked but didn't say anything. "Does that bother you?" I understood that it was different than most people were used to.

His face scrunched up as if he were offended by the question. "Of course not. I just thought I misheard you." He shrugged and added, "It's not something *I'd* personally be interested in, but if they're happy, more power to them. Everyone deserves to be happy."

"You're pretty incredible, you know that?" There was no judgement in his heart. Lennox ducked his head and smiled at the floor. "But yes, Flynn, Fletcher, and Sam will be visiting in a few days, along with a few others. I'd really like for you to meet them all." They were a rowdy bunch and I hoped they didn't startle Lennox, but I wanted to show off my mate and my good fortune to the people who were important in my life.

"I'd love to meet your friends," he answered, lifting his smile to me.

"Thank you." A ding sounded behind me and I told him, "Sounds like our biscuits are ready to come out." I slipped on an oven mitt and pulled out the sheets, which were covered in perfectly baked dough.

"Mm, they smell wonderful," Lennox gushed as he sniffed the air.

"While they're cooling, we'll make the icing and slice the cherries." He nodded determinedly and we got to work; I helped him whisk together milk and confectioners' sugar to make a thick, sweet paste, and then we each chopped the cherries in half.

The biscuits weren't quite cool yet, so I pulled all of the scones from the oven and slid them into the glass display case in the dining area as Lennox practically drooled over them. I offered him one, but he said he wanted to wait for our special biscuits.

A few minutes later, the biscuits were cool to the touch, so we slathered raspberry preserves onto them and squished them together in pairs. Lennox covered the sandwiches in icing (going a little overboard as I just smiled) and we topped each biscuit with half a cherry while the icing was still wet.

"These look amazing!" Lennox exclaimed, clapping his hands together. "But there are way too many for us to eat by ourselves." The recipe made about four dozen biscuits total. "Can we put some in the display case for everyone to try?"

Everything he said melted my heart into a puddle. "I think that's a great idea." I loaded the treats into the case, keeping a plateful out for our breakfast, which I carried to a table in the dining area. "Would you like something to drink?"

"Naw, I'm okay." Lennox was too focused on the biscuits to worry about anything else. He lifted one from the plate and moaned when he took a large bite. "Mm, delicious."

I bit a chunk off of one myself and smiled as the sweet icing and raspberry flavors burst across my tongue. "These *are* delicious; you're a wonderful baker."

"Thank you for helping me. I can't wait to make more sweeties with you."

"Neither can I."

We devoured the entire plate of biscuits in front of us before Lennox leaned forward and asked, "Will you tell me about your time in the Army now?"

"I will tell you about my time as a warrior, but I was never in the armed forces which you speak of." At his confused look, I reached across the tabletop and took his hands in mine. "Lennox, what I'm about to tell you may sound unbelievable, but I swear to you that it's the truth. I just ask that you remember who I am and try not to be afraid." His trepidation saturated the air as he swallowed thickly, but he nodded for me to continue.

I took a deep breath as I tried to decide the best way to begin my story. "Long ago, my people were ruled by a king named Leon. In his early years on the throne, we were at peace, but over time, Leon became drunk with power. He believed that his people were the only ones worthy to run the world, and that all others should be enslaved or eradicated."

"Some of his followers celebrated the idea, but others revolted against it. Time and time again, they tried talking sense into Leon, but he would not hear reason. When he began enacting his plans, an army rose against him."

I squeezed his hand and resumed, "I was in that army, along with Callum, Flynn, Fletcher, and hundreds of others. We were led by a man named Felipe, who was Leon's own brother. We fought long and hard, and much blood was shed on both sides, but we were victorious. Felipe took the throne, and peace came back to our kind."

"We scattered across the globe and Felipe named a Master to each region to watch over his people and tend to their needs. He chose Callum to lead Beckenridge because of his strong moral compass. He also chose me as his second in command because of my strength and level headedness. Together, we care for these lands and our people and act as liaisons to the king."

Lennox squeezed my hand in return. "That's incredible that the king has such faith in you. I know he chose the right man."

"You honor me," I told him with a bow of my head.

"But I'm confused."

It wasn't unexpected. I looked him in the eyes and instructed, "Ask me anything you wish."

"You said you were born here and have lived here all of your life, but I never learned about an overthrown king or a great battle in school. I never even heard about it on the news."

"There are many reasons for that." Lennox raised his brows in question and I took another deep breath; this was where the conversation became difficult. "First of all, the battle took place in Spain, where the king of my people currently reigns. Secondly, it occurred in the days when news did not spread as quickly and was easily concealed. It happened centuries ago."

Lennox loosened his grip on my hands. "I...I don't understand."

"When I told you my age, I was telling the truth; I've been on this earth for nearly five hundred years."

I didn't stop him when he pulled his hands away from me, even though it broke my heart. "Is this some kind of joke? It's not funny, Lachlan. I opened up to you and told you *everything* about my life and now you're fucking with me."

"I would *never* do that," I insisted. "It means everything to me that you trusted me with your story, and now I'm trying to share mine. I've never lied to you and I never will." I felt his confusion and anger rising, and in my desperation to keep his trust, I blurted out, "I'm this age because I am not human. I'm a vampire."

That certainly didn't calm Lennox down. His cheeks reddened as a wave of his anger hit me square in the chest. He crossed his arms and glared at me, and I scrambled to get the conversation back on track.

"I'm telling you the truth; remember how I can carry you so easily? That's because vampires have great strength. We also have great endurance, which is why I didn't get winded on the football field. We can't get sick and our bodies stop aging at about thirty-five, which is why I look like this instead of an old man. I wear kilts because I've worn them since they were invented." Lennox didn't look like he was buying any of what I was saying, but a great idea lodged in my brain. "Watch." I opened my mouth and allowed my fangs to drop to full length.

"Jesus!" He leapt from his chair and sandwiched his face in his hands. "This isn't possible. Vampires don't exist."

I gave him a half-smile. "I assure you, we do."

He gasped as the color drained from his face. "Little lamb." I was clueless until he added, "You're going to slaughter me and drink my blood."

"*What*?" I massaged the pain in my chest that his accusation caused. "Lennox, you know that's not true. Think about our time together; have I ever *once* made you fear for your life, or have I protected and cared for you? Do you doubt that I love you?"

His hands slowly dropped to his sides and he shook his head. "No. I...I know you love me. I can feel it."

I took a step towards him and sighed in relief when he didn't stop me. "Lennox, there are many legends and rumors about my kind that are simply not true. That's why more people don't know of our existence; humans would panic when it's not needed. Fear of the unknown has caused people to create scary stories about us, but when it comes down to it, vampires aren't all that different from humans. We want what everyone wants; to live happy lives with the ones we love."

Finally, his fear melted away as he let out a long breath. "I'm sorry, Lach. I've heard all of the scary stories and I guess I let them get to me. But you're right; I know you. I know that you've taken care of me when you could have hurt me. You've fed me and made me laugh; you've made me happy again. I know that you love me, just as I love you." He reached out his hand and asked, "Will you forgive me?"

I gripped his hand to pull him into a tight hug. "Of course. I know this is a lot to process. Thank you for accepting me."

He chuckled and squeezed me tighter. "I'm just glad that you don't actually want to drink my blood."

Shite. "About that…"

"Oh god." Lennox's knees buckled and I helped him back into his seat.

I took a knee beside him and patted his thigh to try to calm his nerves as I explained, "Vampires eat regular food like humans, but we also must feed on blood to fuel our life source; it's what gives us our powers, including our immortal lives. If we don't drink blood, we perish."

"Ordinarily, we feed on bagged blood from medical suppliers which is unfit for human use; it doesn't affect us poorly since we can't get sick. But once a vampire meets their soulmate, their body will reject any other blood. When I said Fate brought us together, that was the truth too. She knew I needed you to survive."

Lennox looked at me with big, watery eyes as his sadness consumed me. "You just want me for my blood?"

"No, no, little lamb. I want you for your soul."

His eyes widened even more. "You want my *soul*?"

I rubbed my temple with my free hand. "I'm doing a piss poor job of explaining this." I breathed deeply and tried again. "Fate brought us together because we are perfect for each other. Our souls need each other to survive. We are meant to join together and share a beautiful life."

We both flinched when a loud knock sounded on the front door of the bakery.

Through the glass window, I could see the face of Gavin, another vampire from the village. "Oi, ya open? I smell scones!"

Dammit, Gavin, this is not a good time. "I'll be right back," I told Lennox, who looked positively overwhelmed. "It'll only take a moment for me to send him on his way."

"No, let him in," Lennox insisted. "He sounds hungry." My sweet mate was still concerned for others even when his world was upside down. "I need a minute to think, anyway."

"I understand." I gently kissed his cheek and hurried to the door. It was barely open when Gavin pushed his way past me and up to the counter.

"I tell ya, Lach, I'm so hungry I could eat a scabby heided horse." He bent down to look in the glass case. "Loads of scones, eh?"

"I've been a bit busy this morning to make much else," I answered, hoping he'd get the hint that he was interrupting something.

"Hmm, well give me three of each." I bagged them up and made change from his money and he went about his merry way. As he left, two more people entered, and I breathed a sigh of relief when I saw they were Callum and Brodie. I could use my friends' company and advice.

"Mornin, Lach," Callum greeted as they stepped inside.

"Mornin'."

Brodie saw Lennox sitting at the table and waved excitedly. "Hey, Lenn!" When my mate didn't respond, instead staring blankly at the tabletop, my friends hurried up to me. "What's wrong with Lennox?"

"I told him about my identity," I replied quietly.

"And he didn't take it well?" Callum guessed.

I admitted, "I don't think I explained it well; I'm pretty sure he's terrified of me now."

"If anything, he's afraid of the situation, not you," Callum insisted. I opened my mouth to argue, but Brodie spoke up first.

"Can I talk to him?" We both looked at him and he explained, "I know where he's coming from. We're both human and new to this world. Maybe I can help him understand."

Callum puffed up with pride and I smiled at his sweet mate. "I would appreciate that, Brodie. Thank you."

"But you need to eat something," Callum requested. He'd never leave his beloved with an unmet need.

Brodie looked through the case until his gaze landed on the biscuits. "Those are new."

"Yes, those are-"

"Can I try?" he interrupted me.

"Oh, of course. I'm sorry, my brain is muddled right now."

Brodie smiled at me before looking back at the treats. He slowly sounded out each syllable on the tag I'd placed in front of them until he beamed and announced, "Empire biscuits." He'd been learning to read over the past year and was doing wonderfully.

And he *loved* it; he was always excited to sound out the names of new treats I had, and Callum told me they received several magazine subscriptions, which Brodie slowly read to him while they lay in bed in the evenings.

"You make me so proud, m'anam," Callum told him before giving him a kiss to his lips. My friend couldn't hide the love or happiness that his mate gave him; not that he'd ever try.

Brodie turned his wide smile on me and asked, "Has Lennox eaten already?"

"Yes; he helped me make the biscuits."

"Aw, that's so special. I definitely need to try them now. Could I have two, please? Oh, and two hot chocolates."

"Coming right up." I plated his goodies and handed a mug of cocoa to him.

When I reached the other mug towards Callum, Brodie said, "Oh, erm...that's for Lennox. I thought it might make him feel better."

Callum laughed and gave his mate another kiss. "You are a treasure. Do you need help carrying that to the table?"

"No thanks." Brodie winked at me and said, "Don't worry, Lach. Everything will be okay," before shuffling over to Lennox.

"We're a couple of lucky bastards, you know that?" I asked Callum, who chuckled again.

"Trust me, my friend, I know."

Chapter Eight

Lennox

"Lennox? *Lennox*?" I snapped out of my daze to find Brodie standing next to me, and I wondered how many times he'd said my name. I didn't even know he was in the building until that moment; I'd been lost in my thoughts. Brodie didn't look angry, though; he just smiled sweetly and asked, "May I join you?"

"Oh...sure."

He took a seat across the table and slid a mug towards me. "I got you some hot chocolate."

"Cheers." I took a drink on autopilot, barely tasting the chocolatey goodness.

"Lachlan said you made these," he said, lifting a biscuit.

"Yeah, he's teaching me how to bake."

"That sounds like fun." Brodie took a bite and smiled. "You did a great job."

This conversation was way too fuckin' normal after the one I'd just had with Lachlan. I leaned forward and squinted at Brodie, looking for any signs of fangs as he chewed. I couldn't help myself and finally blurted out, "Are you a vampire?"

"No, I'm a human like you," he answered too calmly. "Callum's a vampire, though." I knew as much, since Lach said that the two of them fought in the great battle together. What I didn't know was how Brodie could say that sentence as if he were telling me what he ate for dinner last night. He looked at me curiously and asked, "What did Lachlan tell you about vampires?"

"That they're strong and immortal, they look young even though they're super old, and that they have to drink blood."

Brodie blinked. "That's it? Wow, he *did* do a terrible job at explaining this. Did he tell you about soulmates?"

"He said that he and I are soulmates and that's why he has to drink my blood."

Brodie shot an unimpressed look at Lachlan, who was speaking with Callum at the counter, before turning back to me with a gentle smile. "Let me tell you about soulmates. Every vampire and other paranormal beings have-"

"There's more than vampires?" I asked in shock, and Brodie nodded.

"Oh yes. They normally keep to themselves, but there are many different creatures out there. Anyway, every vampire is granted a fated soulmate. When they meet their mate, they know automatically; their instincts kick in and they recognize us by scent. They know that they've found the person who is their perfect match in every way, and they fall in love in an instant. Even though we're human, our souls recognize the bond, and we fall in love quickly too. So just

think about how special you are to Lach;
you're the only person in the world meant to
be with him, the only person he's ever loved,
and it took him almost five hundred years to
find you."

"Wow. I didn't think about it like that."
I thought the last four years were lonely; I
couldn't imagine half of a millenium on my
own.

"Now that Lachlan has met you, he'll
never love anyone else. He will hold you
above all others, respect you, be faithful to
you, only desire your body, and he will do
anything and everything to make you happy.
Mates are the most important people in the
world to vampires."

"He'll never love anyone else?" Brodie smiled widely as he shook his head, but sadness weighed down my stomach. "What about when I die? I don't want him to be alone." I didn't like thinking about Lach with someone else, but I also didn't want him to spend eternity being lonely.

"I haven't told you the best part yet," Brodie answered excitedly. "When a human bonds with a vampire, we inherit some of their gifts. We heal faster if we get hurt, we don't get sick, our endurance peaks - otherwise I would have passed out after about a *minute* of our football game yesterday - and we gain their immortality. I get to spend forever with Callum, and the same goes for you and Lachlan."

"Live forever?" I repeated quietly, and Brodie beamed. "So...I'm immortal?"

"Well, you *will* be after you bond."

"How does that work?"

"When Lachlan drinks your blood for the first time, you'll get a mark like this." He pulled down the collar of his jumper to show off a pink scar in the shape of a bite. "Isn't it pretty?" I nodded with a smile. "It lets everyone know you're taken. Then you'll drink from Lach and-"

"Hold up." I wanted to make sure I heard that correctly. "I have to drink his blood too?"

"Just a little, and only once. But don't worry; it doesn't taste like blood. The blood of your mate takes on a flavor you love. Once you've both drank, your bond forms. I won't ruin the surprise about exactly what happens, but afterward, you'll be able to speak to each other through your minds and you'll be immortal. Lachlan can already feel your emotions, and he can share his with you. If you're sad, he can cheer you up."

"He's done that!" I exclaimed as I remembered the times it felt as if he was pouring his emotions into me. Apparently, he actually was.

"So don't be afraid of a little sip of blood when you get all of that in return," Brodie said with a wink. "It's a pretty sweet deal."

I felt a little silly for worrying, but I still had one question. "What does it feel like when Callum drinks from you?"

Brodie leaned forward and whispered with a smile, "Sexy."

"Really?"

He nodded. "Oh yeah. You'll be tired after the first few times, but that goes away pretty quickly. But the sexiness never does; it only gets better."

"Lachlan should have led with that part of the conversation."

Brodie giggled into his hand. "It's definitely a perk. Oh, but I should warn you about something; once you bond, you're linked together forever. If you die, so does he, and vice versa. Vampires don't die naturally, but they *can* be killed, and obviously so can we; our human bodies are still pretty puny, so be careful. Lachlan will do everything in his power to protect you, and the whole coven will look out for you too."

It was a beautiful thought. But who was, "The whole coven?"

"Everyone who lives in Beckenridge is a vampire or mated to one."

I never would have guessed; I'd met so many of them and wasn't scared in the slightest. I huffed a laugh; Lewis's hand holding with his 'mate' Sean now made total sense. This whole ordeal somehow made sense; my soul knew it to be true, just as I knew I needed Lachlan in my life. Now that I'd gotten my head out of my arse, I was excited to be his, and for everything that came with it.

"Once you've bonded, you'll have a ceremony," Brodie continued. "It's kind of like a wedding, but it celebrates your love and confirms your commitment to Lachlan and this coven. You'll say vows and exchange a token of love. I gave Callum a bracelet and he gave me this." He held out his hand to show off a blue ring of glass on his finger. "It can be anything that is special to you."

I took his hand in mine and gave it a squeeze. "Brodie, I don't know how to thank you for explaining all of this to me."

"You don't have to thank me; you're my friend. I just want you to be happy."

"I'm glad you're my friend. I...I've never had many."

"I didn't either until I came here," Brodie admitted. "Callum saved my life in so many ways."

"What do you mean?"

He told me his whole life story, from losing his mother when he was born, to his lifetime of abuse and torment at the hands of his father and brothers. He was so strong to have survived, and I was honored to call him my friend.

I felt a deep connection with him and wanted to share my story as well, so I told him about losing my parents and what I'd gone through with Malcolm. By the end, Brodie held both of my hands and his eyes were full of unshed tears. I knew in that moment that I'd made a lifelong friend; we'd bonded over past trauma, shared loneliness, and the love for our saviors.

Brodie rose from his seat and came around next to me. He wrapped me in a tight hug, and I flinched when a growl sounded from the other side of the room. Brodie pulled away with an eye roll and said, "Vampires are *very* protective, even when it's not necessary." He turned to our men and propped his hands on his hips. "Lach, I'm going to hug my best friend, so you better get used to it." I beamed at his use of 'best friend', Callum chuckled at Brodie's sass, and Lachlan smiled too, even though he just got admonished.

"How did you know it was Lachlan?" I asked curiously, and Brodie sauntered up to Callum, hugging him around the middle.

"I know my husband's growl." A deep rumble sounded in Callum's chest when he leaned down to kiss Brodie's lips. When they parted, Brodie asked him, "Did you get something to eat?"

"Aye. I had some of the biscuits that Lennox made." Callum smiled at me and complimented, "They were wonderful. I think you could give Lach a run for his money." My man didn't look upset in the slightest; he just smiled proudly as he nodded. "Are you ready to go, m'anam? I think our friends have much to discuss."

"Almost." Brodie rounded the counter to give Lachlan a quick hug before he came back to me. He hugged me as well and told me, "I'm always here if you need to talk."

"Thanks for everything. Can I ask you to do one more thing for me?"

"Of course."

I lowered my voice to a whisper and asked, "Will you lock the door on your way out? Lach and I have some bonding to do."

Brodie pulled away and gave me a smile. "Of course. But there's one more thing you should know; vampires have *excellent* hearing." I looked over at Lach, who was gazing at me with dark, hungry eyes, while Callum wore an amused grin. Brodie patted my shoulder and said, "Have fun, Lenn." He took his husband's hand and the two of them scurried away, locking the door behind them.

In a blink, Lachlan stood in front of me, cupping my cheeks in his big hands and gazing into my eyes. "Are you truly ready to bond?" he asked in a cautiously hopeful whisper. His face pinched up in guilt when he added, "I didn't mean to listen in, it's just-"

"Excellent hearing," I finished for him, and he nodded. "Did you hear everything Brodie and I talked about?" His guilty expression didn't fade as he nodded again, but I was happy he heard since the conversation was about him as well. "I'm embarrassed that I got so worked up about the blood drinking."

"Don't be. I know it's much different than anything you're used to."

"But it shouldn't matter." Lachlan looked confused, so I explained, "From the moment we met, you've given me everything I need without question. Now there's something you need from me, and I want to give it to you. I want you to drink my blood and bind our souls together forever, because my soul can't be without you. I don't care that you're a vampire; you're the greatest man I've ever met. You've shown me true happiness and love, and I want to spend the rest of time in your arms, doing all I can to try and make you happy too."

*****

Lachlan

My breathing hitched and my eyes prickled. I rested my forehead on his and told him, "You *do* make me happy, little lamb; happier than I ever thought I could be. I've known all of my life that my mate would come to me, but I never dreamed he would be someone so beautiful, accepting, and kind. You're more special to me than you'll ever know." I gave him a soft kiss and whispered against his lips, "I love you, Lennox."

"I love you too."

I kissed him again; it started out slow and soft, but quickly turned into something more. Lennox tightened his hold around my neck and plunged his tongue between my lips. I gripped his hips, pulling his body against mine as I kissed him back just as fiercely.

Our tongues battled, licking deeply and tasting sweet cream and cherries as we pawed at one another. I didn't want Lennox to get nervous from any passersby witnessing the act through the windows, but I didn't want to stop kissing his delicious lips to invite him into the kitchen, so I cupped his arse cheeks and hoisted him up. Lennox wrapped his legs around my waist and kissed me harder as I carried him into the back room.

Any time I kissed Lennox was incredible, but this time was different; more intense. There were no more secrets between us; we knew each other's story and accepted one another fully and unconditionally. The love and need I felt rolling off of my mate made my blood burn and my cock thicken.

I pressed my fingertips into the soft flesh of his arse, massaging his mounds as he moaned into my mouth - the sounds were delicious. Lennox squeezed his thighs around me, digging his hard cock into my stomach.

When I rolled his hips to give him friction on his dick, his whole body shuddered in my arms and he ripped his mouth from mine.

I watched his wet, swollen lips as he spoke, "I want you, Lach. I want you to take me in every way; claim me, bond with me, make love to me. I want to give you my body and my blood. My heart and soul are yours to keep." His eyes shimmered as he pressed a sweet, gentle kiss to the tip of my nose. "Please?"

"Yes," rumbled out of my lips, though it was more growl than word. With Lennox's request, my body was on high alert, ready to take and claim. Primal instincts surfaced, longing to ravish his body and bite his flesh, but I tamped them down; this was my sweet mate's first experience, and I needed to be gentle with him.

I rested Lennox's bottom on the tabletop and he loosened his legs from around me enough to push his hands up the front of my shirt, humming as he fisted the hair on my chest. I whipped my t-shirt over my head and his hum turned into a moan as he raked his gaze over my torso. "I love your body."

It was my turn to moan when he pinched my nipples between his fingers. "You drive me crazy," I groaned as I removed his knit cap, then gripped the hem of his top. I eased it over his head but then jerked it off of his arms so that his hands could get back to their exploration. Lennox bit his lip as he watched the pads of his fingers squeeze and roll my tender flesh. He was half my size, but he could rule my body with a simple touch.

I needed to touch too. I grazed my palms down his smooth chest and stomach until they bumped into the waistband of his jeans. Unfortunately, Lennox stopped his groping to plant his hands on the tabletop and lift his arse up. I hurriedly unbuttoned his trousers and eased them and his underwear onto his thighs.

His beautiful cock was half-hard and swelling by the moment as I pulled the fabric down his slim legs. Once I popped off his trainers and dropped all of his clothing to the floor, Lennox was fully erect and pulsing with his heartbeat. He trapped me in his legs again and pulled me forward to smash our lips together in a searing kiss.

My hands shook with adrenaline as I grappled at my kilt. Somehow I managed to unclasp it and it fell to the stone floor, freeing my hard, aching cock. My boots were laced too tightly to kick off and I didn't want to let loose of Lennox, so I just left the fuckers on.

I pulled Lennox off of the table and onto my chest. He clung to my body as my hands skittered down his spine and onto the round, fleshy mounds of his arse. He gasped when I squeezed them; each cheek fit perfectly into my wide palms.

I tickled my fingertips down his crack and over his hole as he gasped again. It was all mine; never touched by another man. I would be the only one to share his body and give him pleasure. I was curious, though; "Have you ever touched yourself here?" I asked as I brushed my fingertip over his entrance again.

Lennox's cheeks pinked as he nodded. "The showers at St. Joseph's were private; it was the only place I could...*experiment* where the other boys couldn't see me."

I could just picture him running his hands over his soapy body, looking all around him to make sure he was locked alone in the stall before tracing a finger down his crack. I imagined the look of bliss

and surprise on his pretty face when he
fingered himself for the first time. The
thought alone was nearly enough to make
me spill my seed onto the floor, but
somehow I needed more; I wanted to see it
for myself.

I rested him on the table again and
dashed to the shelf across the room to grab
a bottle of olive oil; I didn't have any lube on
hand and I sure as hell wasn't leaving him to
get some, but my lover would need
something safe and slick to help his body
take mine. I returned to Lennox so quickly
that the breeze made the hair on his
forehead flutter.

I unscrewed the lid from the bottle
and handed it to a perplexed-looking

Lennox. "Will you show me?" I requested in a raspy voice. "Show me how you touch your beautiful body." Yes, I was greedy for the sight, but also, Lennox knew what he could handle. He knew what he liked and how much was too much; I didn't want to shock him or heaven forbid, hurt him.

Lennox's hands shook as he drizzled the slick liquid onto his fingers, but I felt no fear coming from him; only excitement and lust. I eased his feet up onto the tabletop and moaned when he spread his knees, allowing me full view of his pretty pink hole.

My mouth watered as Lennox slowly traced his index finger around his entrance before pressing it inside. He whimpered as his digit disappeared, and I clenched my fists so hard, my fingernails made cuts in my palms, though they instantly healed.

Lennox slid his finger in and out of his hole while he chewed his lip and kept his eyes on me. "My god, you're so sexy," I moaned. It took all of my willpower to keep my hands off of my leaking dick; I feared if I touched myself, I'd blow, and I wanted to save it all for my mate.

A long, low whine left Lennox's lips as he slid a second finger inside his hole. His skin was stretched taut, but with a few pumps of his wrist, it loosened and he moaned as he tipped his head back. It was the sexiest fucking thing I'd ever seen, but I couldn't just stand by and watch any longer.

I doused my fingers in oil and pressed a fingertip to Lennox's entrance. He raised his head to nod quickly, giving me a pleading glance that lit my blood on fire. We both moaned as I slid my digit alongside his. I pulsed in and out, rubbing against his internal walls and his own fingers as we both stretched his tight little hole.

His ring of muscle softened and spread until it sucked me in greedily. Lennox fingered himself at a quick and unrelenting pace, but I kept my movements slow; twisting and curling my hand to open him up inside. His moans became deeper and louder until they turned to pleading for my cock. "I need you, Lach," he insisted as his hand slapped against mine. "Take me!"

I pulled my fingers loose as he did the same, and I scooted him to the edge of the tabletop. I poured oil over my heated cock, almost expecting it to sizzle with how hot Lennox made me. Liquid dripped onto the floor and bounced onto my boots; I made sure to use plenty as not to cause my mate any discomfort.

I pressed my cock into him slowly as Lennox's whimpers returned. I was much thicker than three fingers, but his body was ready for me. His hole thinned and stretched until my tip popped through his tight ring. Lennox clutched my forearms and dug his fingernails into my flesh as I filled him up ever so slowly. I don't think he even realized what he was doing, but I loved the sting.

When I was buried to the root in his tight heat, I stilled my hips when I saw moisture dancing in his eyes. "Are you okay?" I asked quickly. "Do you need to stop?"

"No! This is…" Lennox blinked at the ceiling before looking back into my eyes. "This is everything. Please." I realized then he was not in pain, but overwhelmed by the moment.

I cradled his head and eased him back so that I supported all of his weight in my hand; I wanted him to relax and enjoy. I placed my other hand on his chest, feeling the quick thump of his heart, and pushed all of my love into him. Lennox gave me a wobbly smile and covered my hand with his before sending back his love and wonder. My pulse raced and my soul rejoiced.

I pulled my hips back until only my tip was inside him, and then slowly pressed forward, watching in awe as his body opened up and accepted mine. His channel hugged my cock, squeezing my hot flesh as I rocked forward and back.

Lennox moaned as I slid through his walls. He cursed when I brushed across his prostate, and chanted my name when I rocked a little faster. I licked my lips as I watched a large clear drop bubble out of his slit and trail down his shaft.

My hand glided down his stomach onto the patch of coarse hair at the base of his cock. I have his sack a gentle squeeze before wrapping my palm around his slick shaft. I pumped his cock as I buried mine inside him. Lennox moaned and arched his back, pressing his head into my hand.

"Yes," he breathed, thrusting up into my fist. "Lach, it's so good." I jacked him faster, pistoning my hips in time with my wrist. His ass swallowed me greedily and milked my flesh as our heavy breaths and moans filled the room.

"Lach, I'm close," Lennox exclaimed, humping into my hand. He rolled his head to the side, exposing his throat. "Do it," he begged. "Make me yours."

I lifted him closer to me and let loose of his cock to wrap my arm around his waist for support. I pushed deeply inside him and pulsed my hips as my fangs elongated. Lennox shivered as I brushed their tips along his sweaty skin.

I breathed in, filling my lungs with his scent, and pierced my fangs into his flesh. Sweet vanilla-flavored blood painted my tongue. I sucked in a mouthful and Lennox's body quaked in my arms. He cried out my name and his warm cum splattered over my stomach.

I swallowed and filled my mouth again with his delicious blood. Lennox writhed and clasped my arms, repeating my name as I drank from him. Energy and power surged through my body, igniting every cell. My senses piqued; Lennox's flavor danced on my tongue and his scent swirled all around me. The flesh of my cock prickled from the sweet friction of his channel.

Ecstasy coursed through and overtook me. My balls rolled and lifted and my cock swelled. I growled against my mate's throat as a powerful orgasm barrelled through me. My shaft pulsed as I pumped his ass full of my hot seed, claiming his body as mine in every way.

I swallowed one last draw of blood, fulfilling my needs before pulling my fangs from Lennox's supple skin. I licked the wound closed and my vision blurred from moisture when I saw the beautiful pink mating scar left behind.

Lennox's emotions clouded the air so thickly, I could feel them pressing on my skin; abundant joy and love, excitement, satisfaction...and a hefty dose of apprehension. I understood the reason when I found him staring at my throat with his eyebrows pinched in with worry.

"It's okay if you're not ready," I soothed him in a whisper.

"No! I'm ready," he replied quickly. "This is the most special moment of my life and I'm sorry if I'm ruining it-"

"You could never ruin anything," I insisted, cupping my hands onto his cheeks, which were flushed from our lovemaking.

"I just...I don't want to hurt you."

A smile played on my lips. "I promise you won't hurt me. Did it hurt when I drank from you?"

"God no. It was the greatest thing I've ever felt. Well, except for maybe-" Lennox pointed to where I was still buried inside his body and my smile widened. "But you're a vampire. You've got those fangs and you're *meant* to bite. What if I get it wrong?"

"Lennox, you're my soulmate; you're meant to bite too. Our bodies know one another and this moment is fated. You don't have to be afraid."

He took a deep breath and curled his hands around the back of my head, sinking his fingers into my hair. Lennox pulled me closer and pressed open mouthed kisses to the tender flesh of my throat. I hummed in pleasure when he licked my skin in preparation, and moaned aloud when he bit down.

His canines popped through my flesh and when he drew in a mouthful, it felt as if his lips were wrapped around my cock. My body jolted and released another burst of seed deep inside my lover. Lennox tightened his hold of my hair and swallowed drink after drink as he hummed at the flavor. It was more than I imagined he would take, but he could have all he wished.

My mate loosened his bite and ran his tongue along my punctured skin. It was a sweet gesture that warmed my heart, but my body repaired itself. Lennox drew in a quick breath and caressed his fingertips over the mark. "Lach, it's beautiful. Does this mean we're bonded? Am I yours?"

"You're mine and I am yours," I replied reverently. "Our souls and bodies are one." I kissed his lips and smiled against them when a warm vibration settled in my chest. "And now the show is about to start."

Lennox appeared confused when I pulled away, until a bright, glittering light burst from my chest. Then he gasped and his eyes widened, watching in disbelief as a second light emerged from him. They thinned and stretched into shining cords which connected ends, linking our bodies together.

"This represents our spiritual bond. We share one soul in two bodies; I can feel your emotions and share mine with you. You are the source of my joy, and I will always share it with you. I promise to always fill you up if you are empty, and overflow you when you're full."

A second cord of light emerged from each of our foreheads and snaked forward until they touched, forming one. "This is our mental link. It will allow us to speak to each other without words, and will connect us together no matter how far apart we are."

A third and final strand breached our stomachs and connected us. "This represents our physical bond. Our lifelines are now intertwined so that we may spend the rest of time in each other's arms. I promise to protect you with everything that I am."

Lennox's eyes filled with worry when the lights broke free from each of us. "It's okay, little lamb; watch." The cords danced and twisted around each other until they formed a tight braid. One end entered Lennox's chest, and the other burst into mine. The light brightened until we were both squinting from its strength, before it dimmed away completely.

I touched my forehead to Lennox's and told him through our mental link, *"Nothing will ever sever our bond. It will grow and deepen, and last for all time."*

Lennox's eyes shimmered as they looked into mine. *"I'm so in love with you,*

Lachlan. I'm blessed to spend forever with you."

Our lips touched, and we kissed one another deeply and slowly until Lennox's jaw stretched into a wide yawn. "Sorry," he offered, covering his mouth as he yawned again.

"Don't apologize; your body is tired from the feeding, but it will adjust over time."

"Brodie warned me I'd be sleepy," Lennox said as his blinks grew longer. "But I didn't think it'd be this intense."

"It's okay; I've got you." I slipped my softening cock from his body and used a hand towel to wipe down our skin. I'd disinfect the table before baking on it again, but for now, I needed to take care of my mate.

Lennox teetered as I clasped my kilt around my waist; he was fading fast. I dressed him in my t-shirt, which covered all of his personal parts, and lifted him into my arms. "Come on, little lamb; let's get you home." I'd snuggle him in our bed since there was nowhere comfortable for him to rest here.

"What about the bakery?" he asked groggily.

"If you feel up to it, we can come back later. If not, it'll still be here tomorrow." Lennox nuzzled his cheek against my shoulder and I hugged him tighter. His breathing turned slow and deep as he

slipped into slumber.

Chapter Nine

Lennox

"They'll be here in just a few minutes," Callum announced after reading a text on his phone. He and Brodie were at Lach's and my house, waiting for their group of friends who were visiting from America to arrive.

"I hope they like me," I thought out loud. These men were very important to my mate and my friends, and their acceptance meant a lot to me.

"They will," Brodie insisted from his seat on the sofa next to me. He patted my knee and reminded me, "I shot Sam in the face and we're great friends." His words were oddly comforting; if he and Sam worked through that, maybe I had a chance of impressing the group...or at least of them not disliking me.

Another reason that I wanted their approval was because Lachlan asked me if we could wait to have our bonding ceremony until after his friends arrived. He was so excited for us to share our bond with the coven, but he also wanted to share it with Flynn and Fletcher, to whom he was very close, and Dante, the prince of his people.

I was a little intimidated to meet a prince, but Lach, Callum, and Brodie assured me that Dante was a nice, down-to-earth guy. Luckily, I'd gotten used to meeting more people, as Lach had introduced me to nearly everyone in town over the past few days since our bonding.

Most of them came through the bakery, where Lach and I spent our mornings; he was teaching me to bake all sorts of biscuits, scones, and rolls, and I loved every minute of it. A couple of days ago, he told me how the coven split all of the money from the whiskey distillery in the village; he said he didn't want me to worry about money, and wanted me to know that he could take care of me properly.

It didn't matter if he was wealthy or not; I knew he'd take care of me. And even though he was financially stable without the bakery, it was sweet that he still wanted to do what he loved by feeding and visiting with the coven. And I loved being the first to explore his passion with him.

If I didn't meet the coven members at the bakery, I met them on one of our many walks with Freddie. Everyone was pleasant and welcoming; I couldn't imagine a friendlier town in the world. Our football group had met for another game, and I'd grown closer to the guys: Sean and Lewis were great, and Evan was especially sweet. To welcome me into the coven, he made me a gift; a small glass sculpture that looked just like Freddie. I don't know how he made it so lifelike, but it was beautiful, and sitting in a place of honor on the mantel.

I flinched when the front door opened without warning and a man with blond hair and a wide smile strolled in. "What's up, everybody?"

Brodie exclaimed, "Sam!" and ran to give the man a hug.

"Hey, trickshot. I've missed you."

"I missed you too."

A group of men entered behind Sam, and a young man with big blue eyes was shaking his head. "Sam, how many times do I have to tell you that you *have* to knock when you visit other people's homes?"

"Babe, these guys are like family. Nobody knocks when they visit family."

"They should," a tall man with curly black hair insisted. "Especially if that person is you." Sam just snorted, not appearing offended in the slightest.

Lach stood up from his seat next to me when redheaded twins stepped into the room. They beamed brightly and all three of them gave a group hug. "It's so good to see you," Lachlan told the brothers. When they broke apart, the twins bowed their head to Callum with an arm crossed over their chests, but Callum pulled them into a hug of his own.

"It's great to see *all* of you," Lachlan added, regarding the rest of the group. He faced me with a proud smile and motioned for me to join him. "I'd like everyone to meet my mate Lennox."

"It's an honor," a man with honey colored eyes and a thick Spanish accent greeted. "My name is Dante Javier."

"Oh!" I recognized his name immediately. I took his outstretched hand and offered, "The honor is mine, your majesty." Sam snorted again, receiving an exasperated look from Dante.

The prince smiled back at me and said, "Please call me Dante." He introduced me to his husband Ben, Bastian and Milo, Flynn, Fletcher, and the 'irritating yet loyal' Sam, who all greeted me with kind words. "Thank you for inviting us to your bonding ceremony. It's always a wonderful occasion to celebrate when a vampire finds his true love."

"*Any* occasion is good to visit Scotland," Fletcher interjected, "But I'm thrilled for you, Lach."

"You all need to visit more often," Callum insisted. "I can tell it's been too long by these." He tugged on each of the twins' beards, which almost reached their chests.

Flynn explained, "We've been growing them out for the Dunnburgh Beard Competition. It's this evening and we were hoping everyone would join us; that way you can watch me take home the prize for best ginger beard."

"You?" Fletcher asked in shock. "Have you seen this glorious chin carpet?" He stroked his beard and insisted, "You don't stand a chance."

"Does your arsehole ever get jealous of all the shite that comes out of yer mouth?"

"Listen here, ya numpty-"

"I think you *both* will win," Sam cut in, effectively shutting down their bickering. "How could anyone possibly choose between my sexy gingersnaps?" He pet their cheeks and both men lost the tension from their posture. He could soothe the fiery men with one simple touch, and I had a feeling he could get them fired up the same way.

"So does that mean you want them to keep the beards after the competition?" Brodie asked curiously, and Sam bounced his head back and forth.

"I *do* like the way they tickle my balls when they eat my ass." Flynn and Fletcher looked proud as punch, but Dante rubbed his temples and Bastian scoffed.

"For god's sake, Sam."

"What? He asked!" Sam propped his hands on his hips and questioned, "Why am I always getting in trouble? You keep forgetting that Ben and Milo tell me everything; Bastian, I know you like your ass slurped just the same."

Now it was Milo's turn to look proud, but big, broad Bastian actually blushed. "Well, I don't broadcast it in public."

"That's because you're a prude."

Dante rubbed his temples so hard I thought he may start a fire. I'd never experienced a conversation (or a group of people) like this, and it was fascinating. I hoped they came to visit more often.

Just then, barking sounded from down the hall; Freddie had been sound asleep in the bedroom, but had apparently woken up from our noise. He sprinted towards us, sliding on the wood floors and yapping his head off, but no one appeared alarmed. In fact, Ben clasped his hands and smiled from ear to ear.

"Aw, look how precious!" Ben dropped to his knees and even though Freddie was barking at him like a maniac, he slung his arms around his neck. That was all it took for Freddie to turn into a cuddly licking machine. He lurched up on his back paws and attacked Ben's face with kisses.

"Easy, Freddie," I said as I knelt on the floor too, petting my pup's back to calm him down.

"I don't mind," Ben replied with a giggle. "He reminds me of my dog Perry." He paused to get a nose kiss from Freddie before adding, "Perry doesn't travel well, so he's back in the states; my friend Dmitri is watching him. I've been missing him like crazy, but this little guy helps."

"You can play with Freddie as much as you want while you're here," I offered, and Ben thanked me with a pretty smile. "Lach and I want to visit America one day; maybe Freddie can come too and our pups can have a playdate."

I looked up at Lachlan in question and found that not only he, but the whole group, was watching us with silly grins on their faces. My cheeks heated until Lachlan filled me with peace and support and told me mentally, *"Please don't be embarrassed; it fills my heart with joy to see you so happy. These men are your friends and want your happiness too. And to answer your question, yes, I will take you and Freddie anywhere you wish."*

"I love you," I replied, unsure what else to say.

Lachlan winked and thankfully took the attention off of me when he said to the room, "I have dinner prepared in the kitchen if anyone is hungry."

"Hell yeah, I'm starving," Sam replied as Flynn and Fletcher nodded along.

Dinner was wonderful; not only because of the delicious steak pie Lachlan made, but because of the conversations and brotherhood surrounding me. As we talked and laughed together, I learned all about my new friends; Ben was quite the cook himself, and asked Lachlan for his recipe, and of course my man provided it happily. Sam was more than a bit naughty, and though his mates bickered (a lot), I got the feeling that they couldn't make it without one another.

I learned about the deeper stuff too, including Ben's kidnapping and Milo's tough times, and when I shared my story as well, I received nothing but support, and felt accepted and cemented into this incredible group, as if we'd been friends for ages.

Sitting around the table together was one of the best feelings I'd ever experienced; each couple (or throuple, in Sam's case) cuddled close, making sure their mate had enough to eat, and smiling came naturally. Even the biggest, strongest, and manliest vampires were jelly when it came to their mates, and they had no shame in showing their love.

After we were all full of steak pie, Lachlan passed around a tray of shortbread, bragging to everyone that I'd made it, and it would be the best they'd ever taste. The treats lasted only minutes, and all of my friends complimented my baking skills as I blushed and clung to Lachlan's hand under the table. All of this newfound happiness and freedom were threatening to undo my hold on my emotions, but my man kept me strong.

"Okay," Fletcher spoke up after the table was cleared, "The competition starts in about an hour, so we better get going so we can get registered."

"Is anyone else going to compete?" I asked, although looking around the table, half of the men were clean shaven and most others had only stubble, except for Bastian, who rocked a goatee.

"No, we're just going to cheer on Flynn and Fletcher," Ben replied. "And to see the beards in the freestyle event. Sam showed me some online - they can get really crazy! There was one guy whose beard was like-" He swirled his fingers in the air as he whistled, and Dante watched lovingly.

"It's too bad they don't have a hair event," Milo mused as he ran his fingers through Bastian's locks. "You'd win for sure, Papi."

"Or my Callum," Brodie added, and both men received a kiss from their burly vampire mates.

I didn't want Lach to feel left out, but I was too shy to speak out in front of the group, so I told him through our bond, *"You would win the competition for body hair...or just your body...or your eyes..."* I sighed and finished, *"I just think you're perfect."*

Lachlan wasn't shy with his answer; he took my lips in a deep kiss right there in front of his friends.

Sam whistled and figured out, "Ooh, you were telling him naughty stuff with your mind, weren't you?" My cheeks heated when I pulled away from Lachlan's lips, but Sam told me, "That's the best use for a mental link. I like to whisper filth to my men in super inappropriate settings." His admission didn't surprise me at all.

Callum changed the subject by offering, "I can fit half of the group in my SUV."

"And I can carry the rest," Lachlan added.

Dante bowed his head. "That's very kind of you, but I reserved a limousine which brought us from the airport, and it is ours for the night; I thought we'd all like to ride together."

"A *limo*?" Brodie and I both asked. He sounded as excited as I felt; I'd never been inside one of the vehicles before.

"One of the perks of having a bestie who's mated to the prince," Sam smiled while flicking his eyebrows.

"So happy to be of service," Dante replied dryly.

Ben carded his fingers through the prince's curly hair. "Aw Tay, you know Sam appreciates you. And so do I; later, I'll show it by-" he cupped his hand around Dante's ear and whispered something I couldn't hear, though all of the vampires in the room looked a little uncomfortable...except for Dante, of course, whose fist was clenched so tightly that I thought he may break his own fingers, and Sam, who beamed brightly.

"Damn, babe; talk about filth! I'm so proud of you."

"Can we leave now please?" Bastian asked as Milo chuckled.

Callum stood up and told the prince, "We'll follow you."

Lachlan held my hand as our group walked outside, and within minutes, a shiny black limousine appeared to pick us up. It looked a little out of place on the cobblestone street, but it was gorgeous; especially on the inside.

Black leather seats hugged the walls and though there was a spot for each of us, everyone sat on the lap of their mate. At Brodie's request, we listened to music as the chauffeur drove us into the city. Milo chose a station with screeching guitars and screamed lyrics; it was unlike anything I'd heard, but it wasn't unpleasant. It was sweet to watch him and Bastian nod their heads together to the beat.

Sam announced his desire to 'moon' someone out the window, but his mates growled and insisted that his arse belonged to them, and that no one else deserved to see it. That got Sam all worked up and he took turns making out with his men as the rest of us averted our eyes and fell into our own conversations.

It didn't take long to arrive in Dunnburgh. The city was gorgeous; it was a mix of old world charm, filled with stone buildings with towers and clocks, and modern technology, with skyscrapers and sleek bridges. Evening hours had set, and the city was illuminated with lights in every direction.

"It's beautiful here," I whispered as I gazed out the tinted window.

"Perhaps after the festivities, we can explore the city," Dante suggested with a smile in my direction. The others were right about him; he was very kind.

"Really? I'd love that. Thank you, Dante." He bowed his head to me in reply.

Sam tore his lips from his lovers long enough to add, "We'll have to grab Papaw some coffee first," before continuing his kiss-fest. I assumed 'Papaw' referred to Ben because of Dante's look of irritation, and Ben's nod of agreement.

The limo stopped at the end of a narrow road, which was lined with vehicles. If it went any farther, it probably wouldn't have been able to turn around to get out. After we all climbed out of the back, Dante thanked the chauffeur and told him he'd give him a call when we were ready to be picked up, and gave him some money to go enjoy a nice dinner somewhere.

We were surrounded by a grassy field, and up ahead of us was a huge white tent lined with sparkling lights strung inside and all around it. I kept a firm hold of Lach's hand as our group approached and entered the tent.

It was so well lit that it was as if we were stepping inside an actual building; not only did stringed lights drape off of every surface, there were many large lamps hanging down from the ceiling as well.

They illuminated the rowdy people inside; men of all shapes and sizes (and most of them clad in kilts) roamed the area, talking in groups and laughing out loud. They sported beards of all shapes and sizes as well; some were trimmed short while others hung past the mens' navels. My favorite ones were styled; one man had his beard gelled into spikes, while another one was in curled sections that looked like octopus tentacles.

"We'll go register and be right back," Fletcher announced before he and Flynn headed towards the opposite side of the tent.

The evening air was cool and biting, even though I was wearing both a jumper and a jacket. I tucked myself under Lachlan's arm just as a shiver rocked through me.

"Are you cold, little lamb?" At my nod, he pulled me closer and brushed his hand up and down my arm.

"I see something that will help warm us up," Callum stated, pointing to a long table to our left which was being used as a bar. Three men were passing out bottles and short plastic cups. "Will you help me carry the drinks, m'anam?"

Brodie replied, "Of course," before he and Callum scampered off to the table.

The twins returned shortly before Brodie and Callum, who passed a small cup to everyone in our group as Callum announced, "This is the finest whiskey in all of Scotland, distilled in our very own Beckenridge."

"God, I've missed this stuff," Flynn said before sniffing the liquid.

Once Lach held up his cup and exclaimed, "Sláinte!", we all tapped our cups together before downing the fiery drink. Well, except for Ben, who took a sip, gave a full body shudder, and subtly passed his cup to his husband. Dante seemed to enjoy it, though, as he swallowed the second helping.

It wasn't the first whiskey I'd tasted; Malcolm once snuck a bottle into St. Joseph's and gave me a drink, even though I was underage. It was another one of our 'secrets'. Every time I thought about that man, I felt a little dumber for ever thinking that he was a good role model and friend.

"Are you okay?" Lachlan asked me quietly. He surely felt my mood change when I thought about Malcolm. I looked up into his eyes, finding sweet concern gazing back at me. *This* was a good man with my best interest at heart, and Malcolm didn't deserve another moment of my thoughts.

"I'm great," I replied honestly. I was surrounded by great friends and the perfect man who loved me with all of his heart, and would forever. Lach's lips relaxed into an easy, beautiful smile, and I couldn't resist them. I pulled him down to my level and captured him in a searing kiss.

In the distance, Sam's voice said, "Ooh, good idea, Lennox. Boys, my tongue's tingling from the whiskey; let's see if we can make a spark."

I chuckled into Lachlan's mouth and kissed him deeper until a cry of, "Oi!" made me flinch. All of us whipped our attention to a man now standing close to our group. He had a long, shaggy brown beard and an empty beer bottle in his hand. It appeared as if the drink wasn't his first of the night.

"Who let you lot of cocksuckers in here?" He swayed on his feet as he pointed to the front of the tent. "Get the fuck out of here, ya clarty jobby jabbers!"

Bad move, buddy. All of the vampires in our crew growled low and clenched their fists. Flynn took a step towards the man, but Fletcher jumped between them and patted the stranger's shoulder, trying to calm the situation.

"Easy, mate; we're all just trying to have a good time here."

"Don't touch me, ya fuckin' buftie!" The man pushed Fletcher, who stumbled back onto his brother, and Sam lost his shit.

"*You* don't touch my man, ya mangled fud!" He launched himself at the bearded man, knocking him to the ground and bumping into another man (who had been watching the whole argument) in the process. That man kicked Sam in the side of the head, and both Flynn and Fletcher let out a terrifying growl as they leapt at him.

In a blink, the whole damn tent was tangled in one large brawl. Fists and beards flew everywhere, as did hairy balls as men rolled around on the ground, wrestling in their kilts.

Someone took a swing at Milo, but Bastian stopped their fist before shouting, "I'll kill you!" and knocking the guy out with one punch.

One poor sap came for Ben as well, but was of course thwarted by Dante. Instead of taking matters into his own hands, Dante pinned the man's arms behind his back while Ben kicked the shit out of his shins.

Callum and Lachlan stood in front of Brodie and me, crouched low in a defensive stance as they guarded us, knocking away man after man who approached. I flinched when someone touched my arm, but I relaxed when I realized it was just Brodie reaching for my hand. He didn't look well; his skin was paler than ever and his eyes were wide with fear as he watched the scuffle around us.

I understood why violence made him nervous, given what he'd been through. I gripped his hand tightly and called out to get our mates' attention. When they turned around, Callum took one look at Brodie and rushed to his side.

"Oh, m'anam, I'm so sorry. You shouldn't be here to see this."

"I'll take him outside," I offered. I wasn't keen on seeing more blood splatter (or for that matter, more hairy balls) either. "We'll duck behind a car and wait for you."

"Good idea," Lach nodded. "I don't want you to get hurt, little lamb." He jerked when someone pushed him from behind, but he threw an elbow and sent the attacker stumbling away.

"Why can't you come with us?" Brodie asked in a shaky voice, and I could practically see Callum's heart breaking.

"Our prince is fighting, so we must fight too."

"But don't worry about us," Lach added. "None of these arseholes can actually hurt us."

I looked back into the crowd, and it looked like the rest of our group was actually having a good time; Milo was now riding on Bastian's back, cheering and shouting encouragement for his 'Papi' to 'kick ass'. I found Sam just in time to see Flynn and Fletcher each grab one of his arms, which they used to launch him into the crowd while he laughed maniacally.

"Go with Lennox," Callum instructed Brodie. "He'll keep you safe."

"I promise," I replied, and Callum thanked me with a bow of his head.

Lachlan gave me a quick kiss to the forehead and said, "I'll be there as soon as I can."

I squeezed Brodie's hand and ran with him towards the exit of the tent. At the sound of two deep growls, I looked over my shoulder to see Callum and Lach leaping into the fray. Now that they didn't have to worry about us, they could help their friends; not that they weren't doing a great job on their own.

Brodie and I burst into the night and ran at top speed away from the brawl. I wanted to get my friend somewhere that he felt safe and comfortable, so I kept running about halfway down the line of parked vehicles before pulling him behind a red sporty car.

We sat on the grass and leaned against the car doors as I took deep breaths to bring down my heart rate. Brodie rested his head on my shoulder and I wrapped my arm around him, hoping to give him any comfort he needed.

"They'll be okay," I assured him. "They're badass vampires; they can take care of themselves."

He nodded against me. "I know they're safe; I've seen what Callum can do. It's just...when I see people fighting, it takes my mind right back to my paw and my brothers. They're gone now and it's silly to be afraid, but-"

"Hey." I lifted his head from my shoulder and looked him in the eyes. "It's not silly. Trust me, I understand what you're going through. But when you get afraid, just remember that you've got a whole coven at your back, not to mention your very *own* Master badass vampire."

Brodie huffed a laugh and his lips tipped into a smile. "And I've got you."

"Aye, you've got me," I agreed. I never thought that *I* would bring security to someone, given my years of struggle. And though I never believed in fate before, now I knew that Lachlan was right; there were some people we were destined to meet, to change our lives in unexpected ways, but at the perfect time. I was blessed with a lover, a best friend, and a new family because of fate, and I'd never doubt it again.

Now that Brodie was smiling again, I wanted to keep his spirits up. "Hey, look what I've got." I stuck my hand in my jacket pocket and pulled out a plastic baggie filled with shortbread. "I tucked some away before dinner. Do you want a piece?"

"Only if you eat some with me."

"You don't have to ask me twice." He chuckled as I handed him a piece and bit into my own, humming at the buttery flavor. We munched through our treats and I placed the empty bag back into my pocket. The mood was peaceful between us, and Brodie seemed to be at ease. I sighed and rested my head on the car behind me, wondering how long it would take our men to clean up shop.

"Finally," sounded to my right in a familiar voice. I looked to the sound and my blood ran cold at the sight of Malcolm glaring down at me with a wicked grin. I grabbed Brodie's hand and tried to stand up, but halted when Malcolm pulled a handgun from the back of his trousers and pointed it at my face. "Don't...fucking...move."

Chapter Ten

Lennox

I swallowed even though my mouth was suddenly dry. I managed to whisper, "Malcolm," and Brodie gasped. "How...how did you..."

"Find you?" Malcolm finished when I couldn't form the words. "Oh, you didn't make it easy. I've been searching for you nonstop since you left; I took a leave from work. I've barely eaten, barely slept." He did look much thinner than when I last saw him; his clothes hung away from his body and his face was gaunt.

"I've searched every shelter, hotel, restaurant, and festival, and I knew; I *knew* I'd find you." He looked truly unhinged as his evil smile morphed into a hateful glare. "But I never thought it'd be like this. I watched you arrive in that limousine. Who the fuck do you think you are? Is that why you left me? You think you're better than me? I saw you kissing that man. Why would you cheat on me? Didn't I treat you well?"

The man was a fucking psychopath. He'd created some sick fantasy relationship in his head, and had only gone further off the deep end since I ran away.

"You tried to drug me," I reminded him once I found my voice. "You tried to force me to...*be* with you."

"I was just trying to help you relax for our first time. But then you drugged *me*! You stabbed me with the fucking needle and ran away! How could you?" Malcolm took a deep breath and crouched in front of me. "It's okay." He traced his hand down my cheek and whispered, "I forgive you. I forgive you for everything; for the needle, for cheating, and for stealing the dog."

"You hurt Freddie," I bit back. "You didn't deserve him."

"If he would have shut his fucking mouth, I wouldn't have had to," he growled, sinking back into his anger. But then like a flip of a switch, he smiled again. "I would have gotten rid of him, but I thought you would like him, darling. I knew we'd be the happiest little family. And we still can be, because we're together again. Now let's go." He grabbed my arm and tried to lift me from the ground as I tried to fight him off.

"Leave him alone!" Brodie yelled from beside me, and Malcolm snapped his attention to my friend as if he just noticed he was sitting there.

"Who is this, Lennox? Another one of your whores?" Malcolm pointed the gun at Brodie and I immediately stopped struggling against him. I cupped his cheek and turned his head to make him look at me.

"Leave him out of this. It's just you and me now. I'm sorry for playing hard to get, but I'm all yours. Let's get out of here." As much as it turned my stomach to do so, I forced my lips into a smile. I'd do anything to protect Brodie, even if it meant leaving with this headcase. It'd allow Brodie to get away, and I knew Lach and my friends would find me.

"There's my smile," Malcolm whispered. "How I've missed it."

"I've missed you too," I lied. "Let's go home."

Malcolm nodded and pulled me to my feet. "I won't let anything happen to our happiness this time. It'll just be the two of us." He turned back to Brodie and added, "With no loose ends." *Fuck.* As mental as he was, Malcolm was still smart enough to see through our plan. He lifted his gun towards

Brodie's face, wrapped his index finger around the trigger, and squeezed.

I promised to protect my friend and I meant it. My body acted on instinct, lapping in front of Brodie as a sharp *pop* sounded. Searing pain shot through my upper chest and I fell to the ground as Malcolm and Brodie both screamed my name.

"What have you done?" Malcolm yelled; he'd just fucking shot me but was still blaming others. I lay in agony, trying to retain consciousness. My chest was on fire, and every breath fanned the flames. "It's okay, darling; we can still be together." I couldn't fight as Malcolm scooped me into his arms. "I must have you, even just once."

My head dangled over his arm as Malcolm carried me away, and I watched through increasingly blurry eyes as Brodie leapt to his feet and ran in the opposite direction. *At least he's safe.*

My thoughts fell on Lachlan, and how I'd give anything to spend one more day with him. I should've reached out to him for help, but I was caught off guard by Malcolm and not thinking clearly.

I used my last conscious moment to tell Lach, *"I love you,"* and everything went black.

*****

Lachlan

I looked around the tent at all of the men who were groaning on the ground or knocked out completely. The only people standing upright were my friends and myself. We didn't kill anyone or give any serious injuries; these men would wake up from this bar fight like any other.

It was vampire nature to protect people or at least leave them alone; we wouldn't have fought these men at all if they hadn't laid hands on our mates first. Protecting and avenging them were our rights. Enjoying the fight was just icing on the cake.

I chuckled at the sight of Sam at the awards table, collecting trophies for his mates, but went dead serious when I heard a piercing sound in the distance. All of my friends heard it too (not just the vampires), and Callum stated the words I feared; "Was that a gunshot?"

I looked to Sam for clarification, since he'd been shot countless times, and he nodded his head. "I think so."

As we made our way to the exit, Lennox's voice sounded in my mind. *"I love you."* His voice was off; weak and fading.

"I love you too. Are you okay?" My heart raced when I didn't receive an answer. "Something's wrong," I told my friends. We rushed outside the tent and were met by Brodie, who was running to us with tears streaming down his face.

"What is it?" Callum asked as he rushed to his mate.

"It's Lennox! Malcolm came for him and tried to shoot me but Lenn took the bullet and he's really hurt! Malcolm took him!"

"Where?" I asked desperately.

"That way." He pointed to the parked cars in the field.

"Did a car pull out of here?"

Brodie shook his head no and I sprinted to the vehicles at top speed with my friends on my heels. I looked inside each window as I zoomed by until I came upon a sight that seized my heart with fear and grief.

Lennox lay unconscious in the backseat of a gold Focus with his jacket drenched with blood. His injury looked serious, but he was stable for the time being or else I'd be feeling the effects through our bond.

My blood boiled when I saw that he was not alone; a man whom I assumed to be Malcolm loomed over my mate. The fly of Malcolm's trousers was down and his cock hung out. His hands were unclasping the button of Lennox's jeans.

In the reflection of the window, I saw Callum shield Brodie's eyes and turn him away from the car; his sweet mate didn't need to witness what was about to happen.

I let out a deafening roar as I gripped the handle of the car door and pulled, yanking the sheet of metal off its hinges. Malcolm's eyes were wide with terror as he grabbed the gun lying next to him. He pulled the trigger, sending a bullet into my gut, but I felt nothing more than a slight sting. The worst part was the guilt over how little it affected me when my poor mate was suffering.

I ripped Malcolm out of the vehicle and held him off of the ground by a hand around his throat. "Please," he begged as he kicked wildly at my knees. "Let me go."

He deserved no mercy; instead of helping Lennox during his time of need, Malcolm used and lied to him. He tried to kill

Brodie and put my mate's life in danger. Then instead of getting assistance to save Lennox, he tried to take advantage of him. I'd never let him hurt my little lamb again.

I slammed his back against the frame of the car, hearing the bones of his spine snap and crumble. I let loose of his throat and he collapsed to the ground with a groan. I got sick satisfaction from the irony; he couldn't move, but he'd feel everything I did to him.

Unfortunately, I wasn't able to draw out my revenge the way I'd like to; the bastard didn't deserve a quick death, but Lennox needed me.

I lifted the car door from the ground and wedged it beneath Malcolm's chin. I stared him in the eyes as I pressed down; they reddened as blood vessels burst in his sclera. His face turned purple and puffy as he gurgled a final, worthless plea before blood trickled out of his swollen lips and down his chin.

I gave one last swift push, and the metal cut through Malcolm's flesh, separating his head from his body before embedding in the dirt. A dark desire to use his head at our next football game flashed through my brain, but I pushed it away.

When I looked up at my friends, they looked back with a mix of admiration and pity; they were glad I exacted my revenge, but they knew it wasn't how I wished. But what mattered now was Lennox.

I gently pulled him from the backseat and into my arms, quickly looking him over. His skin was pale and wet with sweat, and his pulse raced. Blood still dripped from his wound which sat just below his collar bone, but thankfully it was a trickle and not a gush.

"How is he?" Ben asked, stepping closer and pushing Lennox's hair off of his forehead.

"Hanging in there, but he needs help." I turned my attention to Dante and lamented, "We don't have time to wait for the limo."

"I got you," Milo said before jogging away. He tried to open every car he passed, getting lucky with a black SUV. Once the door was open, Milo pulled wires from beneath the steering wheel. He twisted them together and just a few moments later, the engine roared to life. He could've picked up the trick from his past, his mate, or a damn website for all I knew, but it didn't matter. I was grateful to him.

Before I climbed into the SUV, I turned to my friends and asked, "Flynn, Fletcher, will you do something for me?"

"Anything," Fletcher replied as Flynn nodded.

"Dispose of the body."

"You got it. Go take care of your mate."

As I jogged to the vehicle, I heard
Sam ask his men, "What do you think, boys?
Should we find a cliff to push him off of, or
do we light him up?" I didn't hear their reply,
and I didn't care. Malcolm was no longer my
concern.

Bastian took the driver's seat, citing
that he unfortunately had a lot of experience
with this sort of thing, and Milo sat up front
next to him. Ben and Dante took the third
row, and I held Lennox in my lap in the
middle as Callum and Brodie squeezed in
next to me.

The engine revved and dirt flung in all
directions as Bastian peeled out of the
parking spot. As we sped down the road,
Brodie filled us in on every detail of their

encounter with Malcolm as he clung to Lennox's hand. I was in awe of my mate's bravery and selflessness. He was my hero.

My heart sank when Lennox suddenly began convulsing in my arms, and Brodie burst into tears, screaming, "What's happening? What's wrong?"

"He's going into shock," Dante explained from over my shoulder. "He's lost a lot of blood. Let him feed from you until we can get to a blood supply."

I sank my fangs into the flesh of my thumb until they scraped bone. When I pulled them free, two large drops of blood balanced on my skin. I opened Lennox's mouth with my other hand and stuck my bloody thumb inside, rubbing it across the roof of his mouth until his instincts kicked in and he suckled a slow but steady stream of blood down his throat. Within moments, he stopped trembling, but he was far from healed.

"We need to get him to a hospital," Ben urged, but Callum shook his head sadly.

"We can't let humans run tests on him or witness him drinking Lach's blood." Though we'd bonded recently, Lennox's body was already adapting to immortality, changing down to a cellular level. If human doctors discovered those changes or saw our feeding, it could mean disaster for my people. "We must go to the coven; we'll take him to Harris."

Harris was our version of a doctor; as vampires, we didn't need physicians, but Callum thought it would be a good idea to have someone with a little training in case a human visitor to the coven had an accident or drank too much at the distillery and poisoned themselves. I'd never been more grateful for my Master's insight.

Bastian tore up the road, weaving in and out of traffic without ever taking his foot off of the gas pedal. When we reached our village, Callum pointed out Harris' home and the SUV screeched to a stop.

We all clambered out of the vehicle and hustled to the stone house. I ignored the slight unsteadiness of my legs and tightened my hold on Lennox. Callum pounded his fist into the door calling out for Harris, but received no answer.

"What's wrong?" sounded from beside us. I looked over to find Evan staring at us with wide, worried eyes. He lived next door to Harris and had to have heard the commotion.

"Lennox is hurt," Brodie explained through his tears. "We need Harris."

"He's gone; he and his mate went to the city for the evening." My pulse raced with panic as Evan stepped closer to me. "What happened to him?"

"He was shot." My voice cracked when I added, "He needs help *now*."

Evan gingerly ran his fingers across my mate's wound. "Is the bullet still inside?" I nodded and he took a deep breath before declaring, "I can help him."

"How do you mean?" Dante questioned.

"I...I work with small tools and details and I have steady hands." He nodded determinedly and repeated, "I can help him. Bring him to my shop."

Evan zoomed off in that direction and when I tried to follow him, my legs gave way. I dropped to one knee but kept firm hold on Lennox, refusing to let him slip from my arms.

"Lach?" Callum asked, dropping to a knee beside me and regarding me with concern.

I blinked glassy eyes and answered, "He's getting weaker." And so was I; the more dire Lennox's situation became, the more I was affected through our bond. "Please...take him." I trusted Callum to look after my mate. Callum bowed his head before easing Lennox into his own arms. My heart broke when my thumb slipped out of my mate's mouth and I could no longer care for him.

Callum raced away and Bastian's voice said in my ear, "I've got you." The big man was surprisingly gentle as he lifted me into his arms. We took off like a shot and

reached Evan's shop in mere seconds.
Bastian raced through the shelves of delicate
art and through the back door to Evan's
outdoor work space.

I spotted a brick kiln, benches, anvils,
and a slew of tools for which I didn't know
the purpose. In the center of it all was a long
table. Evan brushed his hands across its
surface, sending bits of glass and metal
instruments to the ground. "Place him here."

Callum lay my mate on the tabletop as
Milo pulled a chair from somewhere, placing
it next to the workbench. Bastian settled me
into it and I took my lover's cool, limp hand.
Brodie held the other, and *all* of my friends
surrounded Lennox, resting their hands on
his body in a show of unity.

Evan appeared nervous but determined as he examined Lennox's chest. "I need to take his jumper off." I nodded my understanding and he ripped my mate's shirt down the center, peeling the pieces off of his arms and exposing Lennox's smooth, slim torso. A tortured wail left my lips at the sight of his gaping wound and blood stained skin.

Callum gripped my shoulder in support as Evan retrieved a pair of long, pointed tweezers. He spread the torn flaps of my mate's skin and gave me a tight smile before sinking the instrument into Lennox's chest.

Ben whispered, "Jesus," in a shaky voice and buried his face in Dante's shoulder, but he kept his hand on my mate's thigh.

Squelching sounds came from the wound as Evan dug inside it for what seemed like forever, keeping his eyes trained and his hands steady. Finally, he pulled out the tweezers, which now held a small mound of metal between its points.

The group cheered, but Evan still appeared concerned, especially now that a fresh stream of blood poured from the lesion. He locked eyes with me and said, "I have to close the wound. Your bond is probably the only thing keeping him alive, but even with it, his body can't heal until the bleeding stops." He tucked his brows in with guilt and added, "I'm grateful he's out because it won't be pleasant, but I have to stop the bleeding."

I nodded my understanding and gratitude, both for his assistance and the warning. Evan retrieved what looked like a metal paddle from a toolbox. He also grabbed a small blowtorch, and heated the tip of the metal until it glowed red. When Evan stepped to Lennox's side again, Bastian put his hand on my shoulder opposite of where Callum held me. I wondered how much was for support and how much was to keep my arse in the chair.

Evan told me, "I'm so sorry," before touching the hot metal to Lennox's skin. Smoke curled into the air and the scent of burnt flesh pierced my nostrils. My torso vibrated with a low growl and I fought against my friends' hold, but I was too weak to get to Evan. I *knew* he was only helping, and doing what had to be done, but my greatest instincts were to protect my mate.

The cauterization only took a moment, and when Evan pulled the instrument away, Lennox's bleeding had stopped, though his skin was now various shades of red and black. "I'm sorry," Evan offered again, "But he will heal now. He'll scar, but he'll heal."

"Thank you, brother," I told him in a weak but serious tone, and he bowed his head.

"He still needs blood," Dante urged. When I lifted my hand to bite it again, he added, "I'm afraid he needs more than you can give him. And he needs it in his veins, not his stomach."

"Take mine!" Ben insisted as he rolled up his sleeve. "I have type O blood, remember? I can give mine to him." I'd never seen a look of such raw pride as the one Dante gave his small mate.

"He may need more than you can give too," Callum interjected. "But we have plenty of O blood in storage." Without another word, he sped from our presence and returned moments later with his arms loaded with bags of red fluid and coiled tubing. He placed them on the tabletop and asked, "Does anyone know how to do this?" None of us were experienced in putting blood *into* someone.

"I'll try," Milo spoke up. "I've never done it personally, but I saw a lot of people using needles on the street. I think I can do it." He looked around and asked, "Does anybody have something I can use as a tourniquet?"

"Here, cielito." Bastian pulled a hair band from his pocket and handed it to his mate.

Milo rolled it up onto Lennox's bicep until it squeezed his flesh and popped his veins to the surface. The tubing had a needle on each end; Milo stabbed one into the blood bag and held the other one in a trembling hand. He took a deep breath and pressed the sharp end into Lennox's arm, right above a bright blue vein.

My heart pounded in my ears as I watched blood drip through the tubing into my mate's arm. Within a few minutes, my legs lost their weakness and my core burned with renewed energy. My eyes clouded with moisture when I whispered, "It's working."

The group exploded into cheers and shared back slaps and hugs. Ben and Brodie wept freely as they held one another, and Milo and Evan let out relieved sighs before receiving a round of congratulations.

Everyone fell silent when I stood up and raised my hand. I cleared the emotion from my throat and told them, "Thank you; all of you. You saved my mate - you saved me. You are the finest men in the world, and I'm blessed to know you. I'll never be able to repay what you've done for me tonight." I would give Flynn, Fletcher, and Sam my thanks as well when they returned.

Callum smiled and replied, "It was our pleasure, my friend," before wrapping me in a tight hug. Everyone echoed his sentiments and when he pulled away, Callum said, "Come; let's get Lennox home so he can rest comfortably."

*****

Lennox

I groaned at the gnawing ache in my chest. *What happened to me? It feels like I got shot.* Memories and fear barrelled into me like a freight train. *I have to get to Lach!*

I cried out his name as I tried to sit up, but pain burst across my neck and shoulder.

"Shh, it's okay," Lach's deep, soothing voice replied. "I'm here. I'm right here with you. You're safe at home." I blinked my eyes against the light until his handsome face came into view, hovering over mine.

"Lach," I repeated as uncontrollable tears of relief and pain streamed down my face.

He placed his large hand on the uninjured side of my chest and pushed peace and support into me. "I know you're hurting little lamb, but you're healing quickly. It'll be over soon. You're so strong; so brave."

His words caused another memory to flash through my brain. "Brodie!" He could be hurt somewhere.

"He's okay," Lachlan answered quickly. "He's here too. All of your friends are here with you."

I looked around to find Brodie, Callum, Flynn, Fletcher, Sam, Ben, Dante, Bastian, Milo, and Evan all gathered around the sofa where I lay, smiling down at me. Evan Freddie was lying across my lap to provide me comfort.

Brodie sank to his knees and took my hand. "Thank you, Lenn. I could have died, but you took the bullet and saved me." He sniffled hard as tears escaped his eyes.

"You're my very best friend in the world and I love you so much."

"We're both forever grateful to you," Callum added with a head bow.

"Plus, it totally earns you a spot in our club of badassery," Sam chimed in with a wink. I smiled back at him the best I could before drifting my eyes back to Lachlan, who gazed at me with love and warmth.

I hated to bring him up, but I needed to know, so I asked my mate, "What happened to Malcolm?"

"He's gone. He'll never bother you again."

"I knew you'd save me."

Lach surprised me by shaking his head no. "It wasn't just me." He explained to me how every last person in the room had helped ensure my safety.

My tears picked up again; I was overwhelmed by the love and friendship around me. "Thank you all," I warbled. "I...I don't know what to say."

"You don't need to say anything," Ben insisted with a sweet smile. "It's just what families do." *Family*. I thought I'd lost mine forever years ago, but now I had new hope and new connections, and love that would last forever.

Callum patted my knee and said, "We all wanted to be here when you woke up, but we will leave to let you get some rest. Our doctor Harris stopped by earlier and said that once that unit of blood is transfused, it will be enough." It wasn't until that moment that I realized I had a needle in my arm and blood flowing into it.

Dante stepped forward and told me, "I'm honored to have you among my people." He crossed his arm over his chest and bowed his head, which I knew to be a sign of respect. "Rest well."

Everyone gave me kind words and gentle hugs before leaving Lach and me alone. He combed his fingers through my hair and asked, "What do you need, little lamb? How can I help you?"

"I just need you. I need you to hold me and kiss my head and tell me that everything's okay."

He smiled his heartstopping smile that I'd never get enough of. "That's what I need too. Let's go to bed so that we can snuggle together; how does that sound?"

"Perfect."

Lachlan pecked my lips before cupping his hands around Freddie's waist. "Come on, buddy; I need to get Lennox to bed." But Freddie responded with whimpers as he hunkered closer to me. "You know he's hurt, don't you, wee one?" He looked back at me and explained, "He hasn't left your side since we got home, acting as your little guardian."

My heart squeezed with love for my canine friend. "I need him too; can he snuggle with us?"

"Of course he can. You hold onto him and I'll hold onto you." I smiled as Lachlan lifted both Freddie and me from the sofa. He placed the bag of blood on my chest so that it wouldn't pull against the needle in my arm, and carefully carried me to bed.

Once the three of us were cuddled together under the covers, the reality of what happened hit me hard and guilt settled in my stomach like a stone.

Having felt my emotions, Lachlan said, "If you're feeling guilty about Malcolm's death, I beg that you free the worry from your mind. He died at my hand alone; you had no involvement."

His care only made the stone heavier. "I'm not guilty over that," I assured him. "I'm glad he's gone and I'm grateful that you took away my demons. I don't have to be afraid anymore." Lach withheld the details of *how* he killed Malcolm, probably to save me the mental image, but I wanted to know. I'd ask him soon and if he wouldn't tell me, I was sure Sam would.

"I'm glad you're not afraid any longer," Lach said before kissing the side of my head. "But what's troubling you?"

"I could have ended everything tonight; your life, our love...everything that's important to me. But Brodie is important to me too. I promised Callum to look after him and I didn't want him to get hurt. I just acted without thinking and I'm so sorry for what could have happened."

"Don't apologize for protecting your friend," he replied in a firm but loving voice. "I couldn't possibly be prouder of you. You put a loved one's life and wellbeing before your own, and that makes you a warrior too. You weren't a lamb tonight, Lennox; you were a goddamn lion."

The pride I felt from him had me bursting at the seams with happiness. But I needed to know, "I'm still *your* little lamb though, right?"

Lachlan laughed and placed another kiss on my temple. "Always." He caressed his hand up and down my arm and insisted, "You need to rest now. I'll watch over you and take this out when it's finished." He tapped on the nearly empty bag of blood.

"Thank you." I burrowed into his side and yawned. Even though I'd been unconscious for some time, my body still craved sleep. "I love you."

I smiled when I received another kiss on my head. "I love you too. You're safe now, and everything is okay." His sweet promise sent me off to sleep.

Chapter Eleven

Lennox

I smiled at my reflection in the mirror; it was the day of my bonding ceremony with Lachlan, and I was ready for our big moment. Well, *mostly* ready; I looked sharp in a Fraser tartan kilt of red, blue, green and white, a black Prince Charlie jacket and bow tie, a white dress shirt and stockings, shiny black shoes, and a black and white sporran.

What I couldn't get the hang of was the fly plaid; it matched the tartan of my kilt and was meant to be worn over my left shoulder, held on by a stag's head brooch, but I couldn't get it attached by myself. As much as I wanted to make my grand entrance into the living room completely ready, I'd have to ask my friends for help.

Brodie, Ben, Sam, Flynn, Fletcher, and Evan were all waiting for me here at my house, while Dante, Bastian, Milo, and Callum were with Lachlan as he prepared for our ceremony at Callum's house. We didn't believe in the superstition of staying apart beforehand, but I thought it would be nice to see each other for the first time at the ceremony site.

When I walked into the living room, I was greeted by a round of whistles and applause, and then laughter when I took a bow and thanked my 'adoring fans'.

Evan smiled and offered, "You look lovely. Lachlan is a very lucky man."

"Thank you." Evan was my only unbonded friend, and I hoped he found his mate very soon; he was a sweet, caring man who deserved so much happiness. "Would someone care to help me with this fly plaid?"

"I got ya, mate," Fletcher said as he approached me. He effortlessly pinned the plaid to my shoulder, securing it with the brooch.

"Hey, that looks just like the one you guys gave me for *my* ceremony," Brodie said as he examined the stag's head.

"Where do you think this one came from?" Fletcher replied to him with a wink before turning back to me. "You're one of us now, through and through, and Duff Coven is lucky to have you."

"Thank you." His acceptance - everyone's acceptance - meant the world to me. "Wait, I just noticed; you shaved your beard." I snapped my eyes to Flynn to find that both brothers now only had red scruff on their jaws. "Both of you did."

"Eh, we thought we'd clean up a bit," Flynn smiled. "Since it's a special occasion and all."

I looked at Sam and questioned, "But I thought you liked the...you know...*tickling*."

Sam snorted a laugh while he shrugged. "Yeah, but stubble burn on my ass cheeks is just as nice."

"God, I love when you're filthy," Flynn gushed before pulling his mate into a deep kiss.

"Oi, wait for me!" Fletcher hurried over to Sam and pecked his throat while he waited for his turn with his lips.

I hated to interrupt, but speaking of filthy things reminded me that I had a question for Sam. I was afraid if I didn't ask now, I'd get busy with the ceremony and forget, so I cleared my throat and said, "Sam, can I ask you something? Brodie told me that you were the man to come to with this sort of thing so I hope it's okay..."

Sam slowly pushed his mates to arm's length, revealing his wide, eager grin. "Is this a naughty question?"

"Is that okay?"

"Oh honey, it's my favorite subject. Let's hear it."

When I sheepishly looked around the room, Evan assured me, "There's no judgement here."

I nodded and turned back to Sam. "Okay, well...when Lach and I are together, it's great; like really, *really*, great." Sam flicked his eyebrows. "But he's always so gentle with me - *especially* since my injury. I'm healed up now and I want...well..."

I wasn't sure quite how to put it, but Sam offered bluntly, "You want him to fuck you straight through the mattress and onto the floor?" My cheeks heated, but I nodded. "Trust me, I get it; I love when these boys go full jackhammer and then fill me with more loads than a washing machine." *Good lord.* "But I can see where it could be different between a vampire and a human. He's probably worried he may accidentally hurt you."

"So how can I change his mind?"

Sam tapped his chin as he thought. "You need to get him all worked up and agreeable. Have you ever sucked his dick?"

My cheeks burned hotter; I couldn't believe how easily he talked about this sort of thing. When I shook my head no, everyone in the room questioned, *"Really?"*, not making me any less embarrassed.

"Well, step one is to suck his dick," Sam continued matter-of-factly. "Guarantee that'll get him to agree to damn near anything." Flynn and Fletcher nodded their agreement. "Then when he's all hot and bothered, just tell him what you need. Vampires *live* to make their mates happy. If he's still leery, remind him that you're not just some regular human; you're a badass vampire mate. He'll hear and feel your desires, and everything will be great."

"Thank you." It was good advice; Sam obviously knew his dirty stuff.

"No problem. And if you ever have more questions, just give me a call."

"I will." I smiled when Flynn and Fletcher told Sam how smart and sexy he was, and attacked him with kisses again.

"It's time to go," Ben announced with a peek at his sparkly watch.

Before I could answer, Brodie spoke up. "I have a little surprise for you first." He whistled and in trotted Freddie, proudly sporting a jacket in the same tartan plaid as my kilt. "I knew you wanted him at the ceremony, and I thought it'd be nice for him to have a special outfit too." He gave a hopeful smile and asked, "Do you like it?"

"I love it." I wrapped my friend in a tight hug. "Thank you."

"I think he's the most adorable thing I've ever seen," Ben gushed as he bent down to pet my pup. "Yes you are. You're adorable."

"I got an extra one for you to take home to Perry for a souvenir," Brodie told Ben, whose big blue eyes sparkled.

"Really? Oh, thank you!" He joined in our embrace and Evan smiled at the three of us.

"I think we better get you to your mate," he insisted gently. "Are you ready?"

I nodded without even having to think about it. "Ready."

My friends walked through town with me until we reached the edge of the field where we played football games. Ben lifted Freddie into his arms, volunteering to hold him through the ceremony. I thanked him and received a round of hugs and well wishes from my friends before they left me alone to take their spot amongst the crowd.

The scene around me was beautiful; the night sky was clear and millions of stars dazzled from above. Lit torches lined the edges of the pitch, casting soft light over the ground. Everyone from the coven stood in silent waiting, dressed in fancy attire. All of my friends were in the front row except for Callum, who faced the crowd. He looked handsome in his formal kilt and with his long hair blowing in the soft breeze.

The skrill of a lone bagpipe's song danced through the air and signaled for me to move. I walked across the field, keeping my steps slow and in time with the lovely, reverent tune.

My heart skipped a beat when I saw Lachlan approaching me from the opposite side of the pitch. He was gorgeous in a formal outfit that matched my own, though we looked very different in them. His jacket hugged the curves of his muscles, and his thick thighs were obvious even in the loose cut of his kilt. His emerald eyes sparkled when they landed on me and his scruffy cheeks dimpled up in a broad smile.

"You're stunning," sounded inside my mind.

"So are you." He was always stunning no matter what he wore.

We finally met in the center of the field, right in front of Callum. Lachlan took both of my hands in his and squeezed them gently just as Callum cleared his throat to begin.

"Welcome everyone to this joyous celebration. Tonight I have the pleasure of joining together my closest friend and his fated love. But before we begin; Lennox, I must ask you an important question." I forced my eyes away from Lach's handsome face to focus on Callum. "In order to become an official member of Duff Coven, you must pledge your allegiance to its people and its leader, as well as the prince of our kind. Do you give your allegiance?"

I spoke loudly and clearly when I answered, "Yes. I'm honored to give my loyalty to you, Master Duff," I looked into the front row of the crowd at Dante, "And to Dante as my prince. I promise to protect and support my people the best that I can."

Dante bowed his head and Ben wiped away the tears from his cheeks while snuggling Freddie. I turned back to Callum in time to see his toothy grin. "Lennox Gordon, I now officially induct you as a member of Duff Coven. You are loyal, brave, and true, and we all owe you a debt of gratitude. Without your heroism, my mate wouldn't be here; *I* wouldn't be here. It's an honor to count you among my coven and my friends."

I whispered, "Thank you," and received a wink in return.

"Lachlan, you've been my dearest friend for centuries; we've fought side by side and I never doubted that I could count on you. You're a pillar of strength and kindness. It makes my heart glad to see you find happiness." My lover thanked Callum, who then turned back to me. "Lennox, I ask that you now recite your vows to Lachlan."

I took a deep breath and Lach squeezed my hands again, this time filling me with his love and support. I looked into his eyes and said, "I vow to love you not only for who you are today, but who you will become tomorrow, and every tomorrow after that. I'll share your passions and your dreams, and always be true to you. I give you my hand, heart, and body because you are my everything."

Lach's eyes shimmered as they gazed into mine. I saw so much in those eyes; a deep love that echoed mine, and a bright future for both of us. He leaned forward and pressed his lips to mine. It was off script, but I didn't care. I kissed him back softly and sweetly until he pulled away with a smile.

Callum continued, "Lennox, please present Lachlan with your token to seal your vows."

I released one of Lach's hands to pull a silver necklace from my pocket. When I saw it online, I knew I had to get it for my mate. It was perfect; the pendant on the chain depicted a compass. I held it out for him to see and explained, "When we met, I was frightened and alone. I really was a little lost lamb; running out of options with nowhere to go. But you found me and everything changed; you showed me patience and kindness, and gave me happiness like I'd never felt. Because of you, I have friends and family; I belong. I'm not lost anymore. I give you this token because you are my guiding light and my compass. As long as I'm with you, I'm home."

As I draped the chain around his throat and clasped it, Lachlan rested his forehead against mine and replied, *"Thank you for this special gift, little lamb. You're*

my home too, and everything I'll ever need."

"Lachlan, please recite your vows to
Lennox," Callum requested.

Lach didn't lift his forehead from
mine; he stayed close and looked deep into
my eyes. If it weren't for Ben's quiet tears in
the background, it would be easy to believe
Lach and I were alone. No matter our
surroundings, my focus was always on him.

"I vow to fulfill your every need. I will
defend you, fight for you, and protect you. I
will lift you up when you're down. I will fall
more in love with you every day for the rest
of time, and I see these words not only as
promises, but privileges. I'm blessed to have

you in my life and you are what makes it worth living."

Without a cue from Callum, Lach retrieved a necklace from his own pocket. It was shiny, silver, and had a pretty emblem hanging from the chain. "This is an eternity knot. It's to remind you that my love has no end. My promises are forever and my loyalty is everlasting."

Lachlan secured the pendant around my neck and Callum placed a hand on each of our shoulders. "Love is a light to guide you and a blanket to warm you. It is a wonder given to you to cherish and hold forever dear. Your souls and hearts are eternally bound as one." He announced to the crowd, "Please join me in celebrating the bond between Lachlan and Lennox!"

The coven cheered and applauded as we kissed again. My heart was full of happiness and gratitude for this wonderful man before me and the friends who surrounded me.

Sam's call of, "Let's party!" rang clear, and everyone cheered again.

We celebrated for hours on the field, dancing to music, laughing, drinking whiskey, and eating a huge cake Ben made for us - he said that it was his gift, and that he didn't want us to have to bake anything for our own party. It was seven layers of different delicious flavors, and there wasn't a single scrap left over.

I met all of Lach's family, who made the trip to watch our ceremony. I'll admit it weirded me out a bit when I met his parents and they looked the same age as Lachlan, but they were so sweet and embracing; they welcomed me into the family with open arms. I was excited to have siblings (Lach's brothers claimed me as their own) and although we lived apart in distance, we promised to speak and visit often. Lach had filled my world with family and warmth.

When the party began to wind down, I asked Ben if he'd mind keeping Freddie at his and Dante's guest house. I hoped that Lach and I would be making a commotion at our place, and I didn't want to disturb my pup. Ben was happy to oblige, and he was one of the first to leave the festivities; tucked under Dante's arm, carrying Freddie, and yawning widely.

"Would you like another drink?" Lach asked when he saw that the glass I held was empty.

"Actually, I'm ready to go home." I bit my lip and widened my eyes in what I hoped was a 'come and get me' look. Lach seemed to get the message, as his gaze darkened and his jaw rippled.

"Ooh, I know that look," Sam said as he approached with his mates. "Someone's about to have a great time." He leaned closer to me and whispered, "Good luck and have fun," before winking. Then Flynn hoisted Sam over his shoulder. They and

Fletcher (who stole kisses from his mate as he followed) scurried off towards the place they were staying, surely in for some great times of their own.

The rest of our friends were close behind, and gave Lach and me hugs and well wishes. We made a plan to meet for lunch the next day; our American friends were leaving in a few days and we wanted to see them as much as possible before they went home. Lots of video calls and visits were in our future.

Once everyone left to turn in for the night, I gave Lach the sultry look once more and ran my hand up his chest as I requested, "Take me."

Chapter Twelve

Lachlan

Lennox's words lit a fire within me. I was still riding high from his sweet vows and presenting our love to the whole coven, and I was consumed by the need to share that love with my perfect mate.

I scooped Lennox into my arms and he held on tightly as I sprinted to our house. I burst inside, kicked the door closed behind us, and hustled straight to our bedroom.

My fingers burned with the need to touch his beautiful body. I quickly stripped off our clothing, tossing articles around the room and even ripping fabric in my haste.

My nipples contracted when cool air kissed my bare skin, but heat burned inside my veins.

I hungrily gazed at Lennox's naked body, visually devouring his smooth, pale skin, his lean form, and his perfect cock. I needed to touch; to grab, take and claim what was mine now and forever. I growled and reached out for him, but stilled my hands when my eyes flitted across the gunshot scar on his chest. It was a reminder of his human limitations and fragility; the exact reason why I needed to be gentle with him.

I looked up into his wide eyes and mentally kicked myself. We'd just shared a ceremony so lovely and romantic, and now I was being the furthest thing from it. Lennox deserved better than my primal instincts.

"I'm sorry," I offered quietly before gently cupping his cheeks in my hands. "I forgot myself."

Lennox surprised me by replying, "Are you *kidding*? The way you hauled me in here and ripped off my clothes was hot as hell!"

"Really?"

He nodded quickly before patting the edge of the bed. "Come sit here."

I did as he asked, with the expectation of having a conversation about what he wanted. What I wasn't expecting was Lennox dropping to his knees in front of me and wrapping his plump lips around the head of my cock.

I gripped the side of the mattress to keep my hands from grabbing my lover. Lennox's pretty blue-gray eyes locked with mine as he sucked so hard on my crown that his cheeks hollowed. He slowly slid his lips down my shaft until my flesh brushed the back of his throat.

He pulled back until my tip was just past his lips before swallowing me down again. Over and over, he bobbed his head along my length, sucking my hot flesh. I cursed aloud when Lennox licked across my slit, and then stuck the tip of his tongue inside.

He was insatiable. He gobbled my cock like it was his favorite sweetie; sucking, licking, and moaning at the flavor of every drop of pre-cum he pulled from me.

Pleasure coursed through my body when his hand cupped my balls. He massaged and pulled my sack as he milked my cock with his pretty lips. Tingling started on the tips of my toes and quickly crawled up my legs.

When I groaned, "Lennox, I'm close," he pulled his lips from my skin and released my balls, and I lurched forward at the loss.

"I want you to come inside me," he explained. "I want you to ride my arse hard and fill me up with your cum."

I was too shocked to reply anything but, "Damn."

"I love how strong you are and I want to feel it. My body is yours; I want you to take it without holding back."

I was so turned on, I wanted to grab him and own him the way he wished, but I still worried, "I don't want to hurt you."

"You won't. I'm made for you; we're made for each other. If it's too much, I promise to tell you, but I need you, Lach."

I craved to meet every last one of his needs, just as my body craved his. *So what am I waiting for?*

I took his face in my hands and pulled him into a hot, deep kiss. I sank my tongue in his mouth and licked against his, tasting whiskey and my own essence on his skin.

I gripped Lennox beneath his arms and lifted him into my lap. I held him tightly and kissed him harder. My fingertips pressed into his supple skin and he sighed into my mouth, fueling my desire.

I stood up and Lennox clenched his legs around my waist as I carried him around to the other side of the bed. I retrieved a bottle of lube from the side table and drenched my cock with the cool liquid before tossing the bottle on the bed.

I grabbed Lennox's hips and positioned his hole over the tip of my slick cock. I watched his face for any sign of discomfort when I pushed him down, but it was etched only in bliss as I pressed inside him, stretching his flesh and filling him with mine.

Lennox moaned, "Yes, Lach," as I sank every thick inch inside him until my pubes brushed against his balls. "Fuck me." I lifted his hips and gently pulled him down onto my cock again, but Lennox begged for more, harder.

I trusted our bond and took a deep breath before lifting him again and slamming him down. Lennox's eyes rolled back and he cried out as his pleasure filled the air around us. Seeing him in the throes of bliss only made me want to give him more. I pierced into him, growling when his internal walls squeezed around me.

"So hot," he chanted as I pistoned my hips back and forth. "Give me more."

I pinned his back against the wall and pummeled his hole while I nibbled on his throat; barely piercing the tip of my fangs into his supple flesh and licking away the sweet drops of blood as he writhed and begged for me to feed. *Not yet.*

I gripped his wrists and plastered them to the wall above his head, trapping him in my hold. His legs squeezed tighter around my waist as I fucked him fast and hard.

Heat crackled between us and sweat dripped down the side of Lennox's beautiful face. His plump lips were parted and whispering my name. Beneath his heavy eyelids, his gaze was dark, intense, and shimmering with need. His cock leaked a steady stream onto my stomach, and the sticky fluid stretched between us as I pounded into him, filling the room with the sounds of slapping skin and guttural growls. My sweet mate needed release and I wouldn't make him wait any longer.

I buried my face in his neck again and bit down into his flesh. A gush of vanilla flavored blood coated my taste buds as Lennox cried out my name. His warm cum splattered up my stomach and his body quaked in my arms.

His channel pulsed around my cock and I couldn't hold out any longer. I growled against his throat and plunged my dick inside him as I erupted, filling him to the brim with my seed.

My hips slowed down and my breathing soon followed. I pulled my fangs from his throat and licked away the last few drops of blood that leaked from him, sealing his mating scar once more. I kissed the mark before pulling away and looking into Lennox's eyes, which were dreamy and satisfied.

"That was incredible," he whispered as aftershocks rocked through his body. My little lamb liked it a little rough.

I eased his hands from the wall and massaged them for a moment before kissing his wrists. No matter how rough or wild we got, I'd always take care of him. Lennox draped his arms around my neck and I cradled his back as I carried him to the bed and lay him down on the mattress.

I eased out of his body before retrieving a damp cloth from the bathroom. Once I cleansed our skin, I climbed into bed beside him and got us tucked beneath the blankets. Lennox snuggled close, resting his head on my chest like always.

"I love the way this looks on you," he whispered as he trailed his fingers along the chain around my neck. The compass pendant lay nestled in the hair between my pecs.

I caressed his back and replied, "Thank you for the perfect gift. I'm honored to guide and protect you forever."

Lennox craned his neck for a kiss and settled back onto my chest. "I still can't believe that this is my life; a beautiful home, great friends and family, and a hundred lifetimes to spend with my sexy vampire mate. How did I get so lucky?"

"I'm the lucky one, little lamb."

"I love you so much," he said through a wide yawn.

"I love you too. Rest well, Lennox; I've got you." I kissed his forehead and pulled him closer. "I've always got you."

Thank you for reading "Take Me"! I hope you enjoyed the book. If you did, please consider leaving a review. Stay tuned for the final book in the "Duff Coven" series. It's titled, "Tame Me," and features Evan's story with his fox shifter mate! Look below for other titles by Jayda Marx!

Other Reads (Free with Kindle Unlimited):

M/M Paranormal Romance:

Once Bitten: Javier Coven Book 1 (Vampire M/M)

Twice Shy: Javier Coven Book 2 (Vampire M/M)

Twice Bitten: Javier Coven Book 3 (Vampire M/M/M)

Release Me: Duff Coven Book 1 (Vampire M/M)

Take Me: Duff Coven Book 2 (Vampire M/M)

Tame Me: Duff Coven Book 3 (Vampire M/M) Coming soon!

Mine to Save: Pine Ridge Pack Book 1 (M/M Wolf Shifter)

Mine to Keep: Pine Ridge Pack Book 2 (M/M Wolf Shifter)

Mine to Protect: Pine Ridge Pack Book 3 (M/M Wolf Shifter)

Shadow Walker: Bay City Coven Book 1 (Vampire M/M)

Into the Shadows: Bay City Coven Book 2 (Vampire M/M)

Magic Touch (M/M Mage)

Daddy's Bite: Love Bites Book 1 (Vampire M/M Age Play)

Bite Size Daddy: Love Bites Book 2 (Vampire M/M Age Play) Coming soon!

Soaked (Dating a Demigod Novella Series) (M/M Demigod)

Rage (Dating a Demigod Series) (M/M Demigod) Coming soon!

M/M Series:

Arrested Hearts Book 1: Gage & Tyson (M/M) *Can be read as standalone

Arrested Hearts Book 2: Chris & Lyle
(M/M)

Arrested Hearts Book 3: Mike & Jonah
(M/M)

Arrested Hearts Book 4: Sam & Jordan
(M/M)

My Everything (M/M) *Can be read as standalone

My Forever (novella sequel to "My Everything") (M/M)

Head Over Wheels (M/M) *Can be read as standalone

Head Over Wheels: Book 2 (M/M)

Care for You (Head Over Wheels: Book 3) (M/M)

My Grumpy Old Bear (Loveable Grumps: Book 1) *Can be read as standalone

My Confused Cub (Lovable Grumps: Book 2)

Beautiful Dreamer (M/M Age Play) (Secret Desires: Book 1) *Can be read as standalone

Lost Boy (M/M BDSM) (Secret Desires: Book 2)

Good Boy (M/M Puppy Play) (Secret Desires: Book 3) Coming soon!

Finding Timmy (M/M Age Play Romance)

(A 'Nervous Nate' prequel novella)

Nervous Nate (M/M Age Play Romance)

Nate's Halloween Surprise (A 'Nervous Nate' sequel novella) (M/M Age Play)

Boss Daddy (M/M Daddy Kink) (Naughty Daddies Series)

Big Daddy (M/M Daddy Kink) (Naughty Daddies Series) Coming soon!

Bad Daddy (M/M Daddy Kink) (Naughty Daddies Series) Coming soon!

M/M Standalone

Ours to Love (M/M/M)

Chasing Jackson (M/M)

Like Father, Like Son (M/M/M)

Valentine Shmalentine (M/M)

M/F Series:

Housewife Chronicles: Complete Series

(M/F)

Luscious: Complete Series (M/F)

Printed in Great Britain
by Amazon

61083794R00241